Journey to Pansophigus

By
Nikki Wynn
Illustrations by Daniel Shaw

Water Lily Press, Inc.
Houston

Journey to Pansophigus

For information, write:
Water Lily Press, Inc.
17214 Hillview Lane
Spring, TX 77379
www.waterlilypress.com

ISBN: 0-9772168-0-2

First Printing ~ 20,000 copies ~ September, 2005
Printed in the United States of America

Contents

Names and Places

Abbie - a young salamander; *Journey's* heroine.

Alex - a young alligator; Abbie and Bub's best friend.

Akina (uh *key* nuh) - a pink flamingo; Gaea's tour guide. Akina is a Japanese name meaning "spring flower."

Boreas (*bore* e us) – Mt. Kirati snow creature; Boreas is the mythological name for the Greek God of the North Wind.

Bradley - a beaver; lives on a river near Mt. Kirati.

Brenda - Bradley's wife.

Bub - an energetic young frog; Alex and Abbie's friend.

Epona the Bog Lady (e *po* nuh) - a swamp creature; lives in the Swamp of Despair.

Harrison Danforth - a gander; hotel owner in Gaea.

Mayor Chordata (core *daw* ta) - Abbie's grandfather and Gaea's mayor; Chordata derives from the Phylum classification of salamanders.

Gaea (*guy* yuh) – Abbie's hometown located in the flatlands near Mt. Kirati; Gaea is the mythological name for the Greek Goddess of the Earth.

Mt. Kirati (key *raw* tee) – the mountain home of Pansophigus; Kirati is an Indian name meaning "from the mountain."

Pansophigus (pan *sof* a gus) – an eagle that lives atop Mt. Kirati; Pansophigus is a derivative of the word "pansophical," meaning "all-wise" or "claiming universal knowledge."

Petros Perregrim (petros *pera* grim) – *Journey's* evil antagonist; lives in a fortress several miles upriver.

Pteron (*ter* un) - a jittery dragonfly that joins the explorers on their journey; Pteron derives from a Greek word meaning "wings."

Swamp of Despair - home of the Weeping Willows and Epona the Bog Lady

Tuwaki (two *wah* key) – a fictional term meaning "earth" and "rain."

Journey to Pansophigus

Prologue

Tiny pieces of wood fell into Abbie's lap as she dug and scraped at the lid of an antique box. "Finished," she grunted, carving out the last letter. She blew shavings into the air and revealed a crude engraving. It read: *A Tribute to Home.*

Drafts of unfinished letters lay in crumpled balls on the dry, cracked earth at Abbie's feet. She brushed them aside and picked up a fresh sheet of paper. "It's got to be perfect," she said and grabbed her pen.

To Whom It May Concern:

My name is Abbie, and I am a salamander. I was born just a stone's throw from here, near the banks of a pristine lagoon, in a place called Gaea. My mother and father were also born here and so were my grandparents. In fact, most of the townsfolk go back at least seven generations. My family, the Chordatas, go back ten.

Until recently, the thought of leaving Gaea never crossed my mind. It was paradise, a place many only dreamed about. There was no land more beautiful and enchanting; there were no neighbors more kind and giving.

But things are different now. Today, I look out upon a barren landscape. I can't change what's happened to Gaea, but I can make this promise to myself: In the days and years to come, when I think of my home, I will not call up this image. I will choose to remember it as it once was – lush, tropical and bursting with color. And I hope, through the small mementos I've included in this box, you will come to see it that way as well.

Abbie gazed upon the desolate scenery. A lone tear trickled down her long snout and splashed onto the tightly woven paper clutched in her hands. She wrapped a finger in her ruffled shirt and dabbed at the smearing ink. "Someday, this treasure will be found," she said. "And when it is, my words must be clear. I refuse to let Gaea be remembered as this wasteland."

Abbie continued.

My grandfather, the mayor of Gaea, is at his wit's end. The past two years have been bleak. Very little snow has fallen on Mt. Kirati, the great peak in the distance, and the spring rains have been light. The small amount of river water that does flow into our lagoon is contaminated and undrinkable, and we don't know why. If something doesn't change, and soon, we'll be forced to abandon our homes.

I've assembled this box of memories as a tribute to the

beautiful land this once was and the creatures that care for it. If we must go, at least this will remain.

Abbie placed the first of several objects, a wood-framed painting, inside the silk-lined box.

The painting, which hung on my bedroom wall, is of my favorite flower, the beautiful Water Lily. They once bloomed all over Gaea. I often plucked them from the lagoon and put them in my hair. It was my own little fashion statement!

Abbie then picked up a plastic globe and shook it with both hands. Her eyes danced as a tiny tropical scene came to life.

The globe contains a mini-version of Gaea. See the bright blue lagoon water and the many colorful flowers? If you shake it, tons of brilliant butterflies flutter about. Mr. Danforth sold these in his hotel souvenir shop. Tourists snatched them up like hotcakes. I suppose they wanted to remember Gaea's beauty, just as I do.

The young salamander placed the tiny replica of Gaea on top of the painting and reached for two color photographs. She held each close to her heart before laying them, side by side, in the box.

The first photograph is of my family (Grandma and Grandpa Chordata, my mother and father, me, and my baby sister, Josephine). We're on one of our Sunday picnics...in the dandelion field near the groundwater well. At one time, Gaea's beauty was second to none, and as the news about its splendor made it to the outside world, our little lagoon attracted more and more tourists, and more new residents, too. With all those extra people, we used a whole lot of water. And when the rains stopped, the aquifer that fed the well ran dry. The elders talked about drilling a new one, but the tourists were leaving, and money was tight. We could no longer afford it. Sometimes we just don't realize how important things are until they're gone.

In the second picture, I'm with my two best friends, Alex and Bub, swimming in the lagoon. We used to race there everyday after school. I almost always got there first...although Alex would probably tell you otherwise.

Abbie paused, tapping her pen on the side of her leg. The day was getting away from her, and she needed to wrap things up.

It's impossible to cram a lifetime of experiences into one box, but I've done my best to honor this land and the happiness it once brought my friends and family. Please don't let these memories be forgotten...

Abbie Chordata

Abbie closed the box and lowered it into the embrace of a giant Banyan tree's hollow trunk. She sat beneath its lifeless branches, nestling between exposed roots. The afternoon sun drifted across a cloudless sky, drying tears that trickled down her pale, green skin. This was Abbie's favorite hiding place. It had calmed her many times before, and she needed its healing effects now more than ever.

The golden-haired salamander took a deep breath and closed her eyes, willing herself to a simpler time; to a place where lush grass tickled her feet and abundant fresh waters fed the land. For a moment, Abbie slipped into a daydream, taking her back to the picturesque Gaea she longed for. She could hear her friends' laughter as they splashed about in the lagoon's sparkling water. Her parents lounged near the water's edge, sipping fruity drinks and sunning themselves. And on the lagoon's bank, just as they did every day of every year, three ancient alligators surrounded a huge toadstool playing a heated game of Hearts.

"Deal the cards," growled Septus, adjusting a beat-up pair of bifocals on his wide snout. "How long does it take to shuffle a deck of cards?"

"Cool it, you old geezer," his pal, Otto, grumbled. "You know the doctor told me to take it easy. These old webbed feet don't paddle like they used to."

"ARRRRRRRRUMPH!" Septus slapped his broad tail on the damp earth. "Just get on with it!"

From behind the quibbling gators a stunning, pink flamingo appeared. "Now boys, life's too short to snap at each other," she said, fluttering her bright feathers as she hurried along a group of tourists.

The old reptiles were creaky, but they pushed their stools aside and rose to greet the charming bird. "Morning, Akina," they said in unison.

"Oh, sit down," she said, her trademark southern accent dialed up a bit. "You're makin' a girl blush." Otto was only too eager to oblige. He put a hand on his aching back and slowly lowered himself into a sitting position.

Akina winked at the trio and turned back to her guests. "And over here, you'll see our exquisite waterfall. It feeds directly into Gaea's Lagoon. The kids just love ridin' the falls to

the water below. Oh, look! There goes one now," she chirped.
"That crazy Bub, he loves to be right in the middle of things.
BUB, YOU BE CAREFUL NOW!"

A nimble young frog turned in the tour guide's direction,
smiled mischievously, and rode a large palm leaf over the falls
and into the deep water below. Akina waited patiently as the
tourists snapped pictures of the joyful scene. "Okay, folks," she
finally interrupted. "Let's move along….and get your cameras
ready. The flowers on the east end of the lagoon are simply
mahhhvelous…."

***

They had been marvelous, Abbie recalled as she

reluctantly pushed her daydream aside. Gaea's endless varieties of flowers had been bright and fragrant and welcoming, creating an explosion of color. But those days were over.

Abbie stifled a sob as she looked out upon the wilting, withered flowers, now drained of their former beauty. Present-day Gaea was a land of dull, brown shades. It was spring and not a bloom was in sight. No furry creatures foraged for meals. No bees buzzed tirelessly from flower to flower. It was as if someone had flipped a switch and turned off the town's life source.

Chapter One
The Town Meeting

"Abbie, you can't hide out all day," said a husky young alligator. "Sulking won't bring the rains."

"Well, what do you suggest I do, Alex," she snapped. "Ride off on a white horse and save the town."

Alex adjusted his beat-up ball cap, swung his ridged tail from side to side, and carefully studied his friend. She had left home hours before without leaving a note. It wasn't like Abbie, and her parents were worried. But Alex knew where to find her.

"What are you doing here anyway," Abbie grumbled. "You know this is *MY* place."

The salamander was pouting again, but Alex chose to ignore it. "I overheard my parents talking this afternoon," he said. "Your grandfather called a town meeting. It's tonight in the amphitheater behind the waterfall. I think we should go."

"They don't allow kids at those meetings," Abbie snapped.

Alex grinned at his irritable pal, revealing a snout full of teeth. "Abbie...c'mon...they don't have to know we're there."

***

WHAT DO YOU EXPECT US TO DO, MAYOR?" yelled Septus from a back row of the outdoor theater. "Leave the only home we've ever known? I, for one, don't have the energy to start over. I'm not a young gator anymore!"

The creatures of Gaea were anxious and angry. They wanted answers, and they wanted them now.

"Where would we go?" shouted a frustrated spider monkey.

"You go where your family can survive, that's where," another monkey screeched.

"Okay, folks, that's enough!" yelled Mayor Chordata, pounding his gavel on a large tree stump. "Everyone just calm down. We won't solve a thing without some order." The old salamander took a deep breath and twirled his long, white mustache. His kind eyes swept the room as he allowed the crowd's murmurs to subside. "My fellow citizens," he said. "Please take your seats."

All but an impeccably dressed gander did as the mayor requested. "You have our attention, Mayor," Harrison Danforth said, adjusting a red bow tie on his long, white neck. "I'm quite interested in what you have to say. As you know, I've had to shut down my hotel now that the tourists are gone. My family will soon run out of food, and I think we're all aware of the water issues. What, my friend, are you proposing we do?"

"Harrison, I know these last years have been tough on your business and your family. It's been hard on us all." The mayor walked from behind the podium to the front of the stage. "I'm not here to dictate what we should do. We need to discuss our options and reach a decision together."

***

From a back corner of the rocky amphitheater, crouched beneath a hidden ledge, Alex and Abbie eavesdropped on the town meeting. In the past, a tumbling waterfall had created a curtain behind which the sneaky duo could easily mask their presence. But today, hiding would be difficult. The falls were reduced to a murky trickle, and the water in the lagoon below had receded to less than half its normal depth.

"Keep your head down," Alex whispered. He tugged on Abbie's shirt, signaling for her to back away from the ledge. "If they spot us, we're in big trouble."

"Shhh," Abbie hissed. "My grandfather's talking again."

***

Mayor Chordata studied the restless crowd. He removed his black top hat and, with shaking fingers, combed his white hair. "I've invited a guest here tonight in hopes that, together, we can resolve Gaea's issues. Please keep an open mind, and let the man have his say."

The mayor swallowed hard and wiped his brow. "Mr. Perregrim," he said, motioning to a dark figure lurking offstage. "Please join us."

A giant human leapt from the shadows, startling the crowd. Abbie instinctively drew back, desperate to put more distance between herself and the frightening stranger. "Who ...who is that?" her voice quivered.

"It's Petros Perregrim," said Alex. "He lives in that creepy compound a few miles upstream. My dad thinks he's the one polluting the river water."

Abbie studied Perregrim as he approached her trembling grandfather. Dark, bushy eyebrows shaded his beady eyes, and salt and pepper hair, overgrown and unruly, rimmed an otherwise bald skull. An expensive black suit hugged his broad shoulders, straining under the pressure of massive arms.

"Wel...welcome," Chordata said. The visibly shaken mayor offered a hand in greeting. Perregrim buried it with his own meaty, oversized grip and squeezed with unnecessary force. Abbie flinched as her grandfather winced in pain.

"Enough with the pleasantries," Perregrim boomed, chewing on an already mangled cigar. "Let's get on with it."

"Mayor Chordata, you've *GOT* to be kidding," yelled an angry voice in the crowd.

"You expect us to listen to the very man who pollutes our waters?" challenged another.

Perregrim ignored the crowd's negative response, lumbered to the tree-stump podium, and pounded it with his fist. The force created a small tremor, which reverberated across the stage, knocking several audience members from their chairs.

"SILENCE!!" he roared. "I didn't come here to listen to chittle-chattle from a bunch of whiny creatures."

Mayor Chordata shook his head and cautiously approached the unpredictable man. "With all due respect Mr. Perregrim," he said. "You were invited here to help us resolve our water issues. Insulting our citizens isn't going to solve anything."

"WHAT water issues!" Petros barked, focusing his steely gaze on the mayor. "So your water is a little brackish. What's the big deal?"

"Mr. Perregrim, please," the mayor replied, his fear temporarily replaced by a wave of fury. "Our water is vanishing before our eyes. What remains is green and slimy because you, sir, are pumping disgusting waste into the river. Your sludge is killing our fish and plant life, and many of Gaea's citizens have grown ill from drinking the foul water. If the situation isn't resolved soon, we'll have to abandon our beloved town."

The mayor paused for a moment, infuriated by the man's arrogant smirk. "All we ask, Mr. Perregrim, is that you stop polluting the river water and stop restricting its flow."

"NONSENSE!" Petros howled.

***

The riveting drama held Abbie and Alex spellbound, until a loud thump from behind diverted their attention. Alex covered Abbie's snout to stifle her startled scream. Their friend, Bub, had arrived, unceremoniously.

"Bub! What are you doing?" Alex hissed through rows of clenched teeth. "You scared us half to death."

The young frog flashed an infectious grin and hopped between his two pals. "I just wanted to see what was up. You guys left without telling me where you were going."

"Keep your voice down," Abbie whispered. She grabbed Bub by the suspenders and pulled him to the ground and out of sight. "You're too young to understand what's happening anyway, Bub. This meeting is for adults."

"You're not adults," Bub grumbled. "And just because I'm younger doesn't mean I don't know what's going on. I mean..."

"Geez, Bub," Alex interrupted, covering his nostrils. "What is that smell? Have you been eating onions again? Your breath stinks!"

"Be quiet, both of you!" Abbie insisted. "Bub, if you're going to hang around, put a sock in it. Understand?" The frog nodded and yanked a half eaten onion from his pants pocket. He took a large, crunching bite.

"Shhhh. Listen up," said Abbie. "That horrible man is speaking again."

***

"You have *absolutely no proof* that I'm poisoning your water," Perregrim bellowed. "And I don't plan on spending one red cent to clean it up. You're on your own with this one, Chordata."

Perregrim turned to face the stunned audience. His unruly hair stood on end and his face darkened to the color of smoldering hot coals. "Don't you pond-dwellers even *TRY* to fight me on this," he threatened. "You don't want to tangle with Petros Perregrim. If you can't handle a few changes in your environment, then you need to GET OUT!!"

Perregrim threw his head back and howled with

laughter. He then turned to leave, kicking a chair out of his way, sending it hurling towards the crowd. The town's creatures scattered to avoid the flying object and watched, defeated, as the horrible man disappeared into the night.

Chapter Two
A Glimmer of Hope

Mayor Chordata remained silent for several minutes, gathering his wits. He fought the lump in his throat and lifted his weary head. "My fellow Gaeans, I'm afraid the time has come to leave our beloved home. Petros Perregrim is much too powerful for us to fight." Chordata fell silent again, composing himself for what he must say next. "We've lived a wonderful life in Gaea, but there is nothing left for us here. We must put the safety of our families ahead of our pride."

The crowd hung their heads. The mayor was right. They were defenseless against the demented Perregrim.

"We must pack our belongings and prepare to find a new home," the mayor continued. "Our emergency supplies are quickly dwindling. We should be ready to leave in seven days."

***

Abbie was shocked by her grandfather's words.

"No!" Tears streamed down the salamander's flushed cheeks. "We can't leave Gaea, Alex. It's our home."

"We don't have a choice, Abbie.   You heard your grandfather. We're no match for Petros Perregrim."

"Says who?" Bub interrupted. "I mean, c'mon, can't we at least give it a shot?"

Alex turned to the frustrated frog. "Bub, I know you don't understand this yet, but things aren't always that simple. Sometimes you just don't win."

"But we haven't even tried," Bub replied. A full moon cast eerie shadows on Gaea's thirsty lagoon as the frog hastily hopped to keep up with his pals, now heading for home. "There's got to be something we can do. We can't just give up. Coach Collins said to never give up. If you lose, you should lose trying..."

"BUB, we get it!" said Abbie. "It's just not realistic. This isn't a game of stickball."

From behind a grove of wilting banana trees, a soft voice floated toward the group. "Well, there might be one option," it cooed.

The trio spied a flutter of pink feathers and the glint of rhinestones in the shadows.

"Akina, is that you?" Abbie asked.

"Yes, dear," the flamingo replied, revealing herself to the group. Her usually impeccable attire was muddied from lack of washing, but the tour guide held her head high. "Legend has it that an eagle at the top of Mt. Kirati is all-knowin'," she said. "Perhaps he has the answers we're needin'. And like little Bub said, it's worth a try."

"Let's do it!" Bub hopped about ecstatically. "Let's go

now!"

"Hold your horses, Bub," said Abbie. "We don't even know if this mysterious eagle exists. And besides, we only have seven days to reach Mt. Kirati's summit. That's near impossible."

"I've heard my folks talk about him," Alex said. "His name is Pansophigus. He's real. I'm sure of it." Alex turned to the pessimistic salamander. His tail thumped the dry earth, kicking up puffs of dust. "Let's do this, Abbie. What bad could possibly come of it?"

"Hmmm. Let's see," she replied. "You mean besides being grounded until we're too old to care anymore?"

Alex smiled. "At least we'd be grounded in Gaea."

Abbie sighed. "Alright, you win. But if we do this, we've got to be prepared. We need to pack some essentials...food, water, proper gear...and we need to do it without being noticed. If our parents get wind of our plans, they'll never let us go."

"Akina," Alex said to the beautiful flamingo. "It's not right to ask you to keep this from our folks, but we don't have a choice."

"I don't know, kids," Akina said, suddenly reluctant to send the little crew off on such a dangerous journey. "I'm having second thoughts. What if ya get hurt or run outta nourishment? How will I know you're okay? I'll just nevah forgive myself if something happens to you precious angels."

"I've got something that'll ease your mind, Akina! Take a look at this!" Bub exclaimed, tossing a pocket-sized black gadget in Akina's direction.

"What's this?" Akina asked. She rolled the strange device around on her wingtips before holding it up to her bejeweled spectacles for closer inspection.

"It's a tracking device," Bub confidently replied. "I've been tinkering with it for over a year."

"Tadpole," Alex exclaimed, staring at Bub in disbelief. "You never told me you were into this sort of thing."

"I didn't tell anyone," Bub said. "And don't call me tadpole. I'm not a kid anymore."

"Right," Alex chuckled. "So, *Bub*, how does this tracking device work? Or more importantly, does it work?"

"Of course it does," said Bub. "I'll show you." He snatched the device from Akina's feathered grip, and held it above his head, directly in the path of a brilliant moonbeam.

"It's powered by sunlight or moonlight," he explained, lowering the device for all to view. "Just sixty seconds of exposure will keep it charged for hours."

Bub then pointed at one of two red buttons on the device's face. "This switch triggers the tracking mechanism. The other button is the distress signal."

"Where does it send the signal?" Alex asked.

"Good question, my scaly friend," Bub grinned. He pulled an identical gadget from his back pocket and handed it to Akina.

"When you press this button, Akina, it tells you where the other device is located. See the map?" he said, pointing to a blinking dot. "That's Gaea. And further north...right there...is Mt. Kirati. If we get into trouble, we'll trigger the distress signal. You'll know right where to find us."

Abbie and Alex stared at their pesky little pal, amazed at his creation.

"Well, Bub, that's really somethin'. It takes a big load off my mind," said Akina. "Now go pack up, my sweet ones, but drop by my place before leavin'. You'll need bottled water for the trip. You can only last a few days without it, and who knows how long you'll be gone. Now skedaddle before I start havin' second thoughts again!"

Chapter Three
The Flying Ace

Just after dawn, Abbie, Alex and Bub met in a lonely meadow on the outskirts of town. Their backpacks were full and their spirits were high as they prepared to depart on the arduous journey north.

"We'll follow the river to the base of the mountain," Alex explained, unfolding a map he'd found in his father's roll top desk. "It may not be the quickest route, but it's the safest."

Bub clamped the tracking device to his backpack and bolted for the river.

"Slow down, Bub," Abbie cautioned. "Let's keep each other in sight at all times. Petros Perregrim's compound isn't far from here, so we need to take cover in the trees alongside the river. That creepy old man is unpredictable. Who knows what he'll do if he catches us trespassing."

Bub reluctantly slowed his pace and the three headed north throughout the morning and into the early afternoon.

"Alex, look. The river is almost pure sludge here," Abbie said as the weary travelers stopped to rest along its bank. "Perregrim's compound must be nearby."

"There's a bluff up ahead," Alex replied. "Let's climb it and check things out."

"I'll go first!" Bub said, hopping upriver.

Abbie and Alex scampered after him, concerned that the excited frog might reveal their whereabouts.

"Careful, Bub," Abbie warned. "Remember to stay hidden. Head for that thicket of trees on the bluff."

The trio stayed low to avoid detection and stopped to catch their breath when they reached their destination.

"That big tree over there, let's climb it to get a better view of the valley," Alex said, pointing at an ancient oak, bent and twisting toward the valley floor. Bub jumped on a gnarly branch and began his ascent. Alex and Abbie followed close behind, careful not to rustle the dry leaves.

"Bub, that's high enough," Abbie whispered. "Stop right there. You're making me nervous."

"Nervous? You don't know what nervous is, little lady," an erratic flying object squealed as it buzzed by.

"Who is that? Who said that?" Abbie yelped, concerned that they had been discovered. She whipped her head back and forth, swatting at a colorful blur as it raced past her head.

"Watch it!" a tiny, irritated voice barked. "You could hurt someone swingin' at 'em like that."

"Well, if you don't quit buzzing around, I'm going to fall out of this tree," Abbie yelped. "Slow down and show yourself!"

An autumn-colored dragonfly suddenly appeared before her, its multiple wings a blur of rapid motion. A leather-strapped cap and goggles sat above the insect's furrowed brow.

Its large, reflective eyes flickered with agitation.

"Are you fools crazy? What are you doing here?" The dragonfly wiped away tiny beads of sweat with a green aviator scarf. "Petros Perregrim and his army of trash-heaps are just below, at the base of the cliff. If they spot you, you're in big trouble."

The trio turned in unison toward the valley, witnessing for the first time the true wickedness of Perregrim's compound. High above, a flock of black crows circled. And below, an army of heinous creatures stood in morphing lines, their dripping bodies blending together as they stood guard on Perregrim's giant fortress.

"Whoa," Bub croaked, his eyes wide with amazement.

"Look at the big pipe coming out of the ground." Alex

pointed toward the far end of the compound. "It's pouring sludge directly into the river. I'd bet a week's allowance that's the source of Gaea's pollution."

"Well, Pteron ain't sticking around to find out," the dragonfly exclaimed, shivering violently as he perched on a thin branch. "This is one bug that plans on seeing tomorrow."

"So your name's Pteron," said Abbie.

The insect nodded and readied his iridescent wings for flight. "Perregrim is polluting all of our waters, missy. But you're not gonna catch me entering some creepy swamp in search of miracles." The dragonfly hovered in the still air. He was poised for takeoff.

"Wait a minute!" Abbie cried. "What do you mean? What creepy swamp? And what miracles are you talking about?"

"Don't even think it, gal," Pteron replied, tugging a pair of huge goggles over his bulging eyes. "You're not gonna get me involved. Uh uh. Not a chance."

Alex shimmied down a tree limb to confront the agitated Pteron. "Look, dragonfly, if you know something; if you have information about how we can clear up this mess, spit it out. Our town's survival depends on it."

"That swamp business I mentioned; it's all a bunch of malarkey," Pteron replied, diverting his eyes. "It's an old wives tale and not worth repeating….so…anyway…lovely to meet you folks, but I'm afraid I've got to head out."

"Hold it right there!" Alex growled. He grabbed Pteron's scarf and held the squirming dragonfly inches from his long snout. "Get comfortable, Ace. You're about to tell us everything you know."

Chapter Four
The Antidote

"What is Petros Perregrim up to?" Alex quizzed the edgy dragonfly. "What kind of waste is he pumping into the river?"

"For the last time," Pteron squealed. *"I don't know!* We can assume, of course, that whatever it is can't be good. Why else would he need those rancid guards?"

"Well, if you don't know," Abbie grumbled, "then what is all this babble about swamps and miracles?"

"I was just running my mouth..."

"PTERON!" Alex roared. The nervous insect buried his head behind his wings. "You know something. Now out with it!"

"Alright, alright," Pteron whined. He raised a wing and cautiously peered up at the determined alligator. "Perregrim plans to take over Mt. Kirati and the foothills. That includes Gaea, and my home, too. I overheard a couple of his guards talking. They said he was brewing some kind of mind-control potion."

"What does this mind-control stuff have to do with the swamp?" Abbie pushed. She was quickly losing patience with the spineless dragonfly.

"Well, if you'd quit interrupting," Pteron huffed.

"I'm warning you, Ace," Alex tightened his grip on the dragonfly. "Keep talking and be quick about it. We don't have time to waste."

"I missed part of the conversation," Pteron whimpered. "The soldiers smelled so awful I had to catch a breath of fresh air. When I returned, the goons were bragging about some foolproof plan. Then they started whispering, so I had to move in closer. The smell was almost unbearable."

"Get to the point!" Alex hissed, smothering Pteron with a burst of hot alligator breath.

Pteron turned his head and closed his eyes. "Back it up, gator. I can't think with that snout full of teeth in my face."

Abbie placed a hand on Alex's shoulder. Her eyes pleaded with him to calm down, and Alex soon loosened his grip on the dragonfly. "You have one minute," he warned.

"Alright, geez," Pteron said. "Where was I? Oh, right. The guards were discussing Perregrim's plan. They said the only antidote to his potion was weeping willow tears."

"Weeping willow tears!" Abbie exclaimed. "Where in the world are we going to find weeping willow tears?"

"That's where the swamp comes in…the *Swamp of Despair,*" Pteron shivered. "It's the only place around here that weeping willows grow. But no one is crazy enough to enter that mossy trap."

"We'll go!" Bub croaked. "We've got to find that antidote."

"Not so fast, frog," Pteron said, shuddering at the thought. "That swamp is full of awful creatures, and from what I hear, those who enter, don't come out. You ain't gonna find me poking around in a place like that."

"You don't have a choice, bug," Alex said.

"I'm not gonna do it," Pteron buzzed. "So put that thought right out of your mind, gator."

"Like it or not, my little winged friend," Alex said, tightening his grip on the dragonfly. "We're all in this together. You've got two choices. Either lead us into the swamp or join us in confronting Petros Perregrim now."

Chapter Five
The Swamp of Despair

"This is ridiculous," Pteron said, shaking uncontrollably as the group stood wide-eyed at the edge of the dark swamp. "Even if we collect the willow tears, we have no proof they'll reverse the effects of Perregrim's potion."

"Don't worry about the details, Ace. Just lead the way," Alex barked. "And don't go too fast. Visibility is bad. We need to stick together."

Alex grabbed Abbie's hand, and she reached out for Bub. Pteron, seeking shelter, dove for Bub's backpack and struggled to wedge his long torso inside. After much effort, he was sufficiently hidden. Only his bulbous eyes remained visible, peeking nervously from beneath the pack's top flap.

Alex reached in and yanked out the neurotic dragonfly. "Pteron," he said, "how do you plan on leading us if you're hiding out? It's time to put on your game face, buddy. Get moving."

Pteron glared at his tormenter. "I can't fly very well with you clutching my wings, now can I?"

Alex grinned. "Don't try anything cute, Ace. I'll be

watching you." He released Pteron, and the dragonfly cautiously took flight, leading the group into the *Swamp of Despair's* murky grip.

"The willows are located about a quarter-mile east of Epona's Gate," Pteron's voice quivered.

"Where's Epona's Gate?" Abbie asked. Goose bumps crept up her slender tail.

"Straight ahead," said Pteron, pointing toward an expanse of stagnant, muddy water.

Abbie gingerly stuck a foot into the dark soup. "Ouch!" she yelped, jumping back. A dark, red crawfish hung from her big toe, its two claws firmly clamped.

"Let go!" she howled.

"Not until you leave my swamp, missy," the irritated crustacean snapped.

"Mmmm, what do we have here?" Alex beamed, his tongue sweeping across his long snout. "Crawdad, my favorite meal. Tastes just like lobster, but it takes a bunch of these boys to fill a gator's belly."

The crawdad's beady eyes grew large as Alex approached. Sensing danger, he unclamped his claws, dropped into the murky water, and burrowed deep into the swamp's muddy bottom.

"Alex, you hate crawdad," Abbie said as she rubbed her throbbing toe.

"Yeah, but I'm pretty sure he didn't know that," Alex grinned. "Now, let's get going. Bub, follow Abbie. I'll bring up the rear. See those stones ahead?" he said, pointing at dozens

of shiny objects scattered across the foggy swamp. "They're close enough together to hop from one to the next. It'll keep us out of the muck."

Abbie hopped to the first stone with ease, gaining confidence to proceed at a quicker pace. Bub ignored Alex's suggestion and dove into the cloudy water.

"What's wrong with that foolish amphibian," Pteron grumbled. "He'll have us all spotted, splashing around like that."

"Tadpole!" Alex yelled. "Slow down, little buddy, and use the stones."

"Dimwits," Pteron muttered. "There's no chance of escaping Epona with this crazy group."

Bub pulled himself onto a stone and carelessly leapt through the damp air toward another.

"Bub!" Abbie screamed. "Watch your…"

Her warning came too late. Bub belly-flopped back into the dingy swamp water. He popped up immediately, sputtering and dripping with moss.

"Wow. What happened?" he croaked. "That stone just disappeared."

"They're not stones," Pteron said, buzzing nervously above his companions. "They're turtles…snapping turtles. And you're all standing on them."

"Use them anyway, Bub," Abbie insisted. She had successfully made it across and was standing on solid ground. "But walk softly. Try not to upset them."

"Okay, but what's that?" Bub asked, pointing toward a

ripple moving in his direction.

"Bub, listen to me," Abbie's voice quivered as she spotted the approaching danger. "Get to the next turtle...now."

Pteron was less coy. "Run!" he shouted. "Anaconda! Anaconda! Run for your life!"

Abbie shot an angry look in Pteron's direction but quickly realized the monstrous snake was closing in fast. She decided the crazy dragonfly might have the right idea.

"Hurry, Bub!" she joined in. "Run...swim... whatever you have to do. Just get over here now!"

Bub scrambled to regain his footing, but it was useless. The turtles scattered as the giant anaconda drew near. Desperate, Bub dove deep into the cloudy water and used the spongy swamp bottom as a launching pad. The agile frog soared out of the water, over the fleeing turtles, and into Abbie's outstretched arms. Pteron circled above, his tiny heart thumping against his chest.

"I can't do this," he cried, furiously flapping his wings. "That frog is trouble waiting to happen. If we don't get out of this swamp, we're doomed. I'm heading for sunlight."

"Oh, no you're not," a gurgling voice muttered from the darkness of the swamp's foliage. "Who dares to trespass in my waters?"

"Oh, no!" Pteron shrieked. "It's Epona! We're history. It's over!"

"What? Who's Epona?" Abbie asked. She looked around but saw only foggy swamp.

"Shhhh. Not so loud." Pteron disappeared once more

into Bub's backpack. He popped his trembling head out long enough to say, "We have to get out of here! No one meets Epona the Bog Lady and lives to tell about it"

"How do you know?" Bub argued.

"I just know!" Pteron yelped, tangling his wings in the contents of the frog's pack. "Now GO!"

"Not so fast!" the sinister voice hissed. Two penetrating red eyes pierced the haze. Swamp water bubbled and boiled beneath the mysterious figure.

"What...what is that," Abbie gasped. She could barely make out a dark, tattered cape and a wild tuft of long, mossy hair.

"You good-for-nothing little rogues," the Bog Lady wheezed. "You dare trespass in my swamp? This is the end of the road...for all of you!"

Chapter Six
Epona's Wrath

Pteron, fully burrowed in Bub's backpack, squeezed his eyes shut and prepared for what he knew were his final moments.

Alex, Abbie, and Bub, with no obvious escape route, stood frozen in Epona's presence.

"Out of my way, snake!" the bog lady screamed, walloping a still-determined anaconda with her knotty, twisted staff. The chastised snake hissed, but dutifully retreated. Epona focused again on the frightened intruders. "These three varmints, and that meddlesome dragonfly, are mine." Her blazing eyes glowed behind a mass of unruly hair and bore into Abbie.

"I've always enjoyed a tasty salamander," Epona cackled. Her eyes danced as she rolled twig-like hands together in anticipation. Abbie gasped and retreated. She stumbled over a large tree root and landed hard on the soggy earth.

Alex instinctively jumped between Abbie and her tormenter. "Back off, swamp thing, or else!" he yelled.

"Or else what?" she wheezed. Her chilling taunt echoed

through the swamp.

Alex stood his ground. "Bub, help Abbie," he ordered. "Get her out of here. I'll cover your back. When you're in the clear, hit the distress signal on the tracking device. Let Akina know where we are."

"We can't go without you, Alex," Bub protested as he helped Abbie to her feet. She was dazed, but unhurt.

"Both of you go, now!" Alex demanded. "I'll take care of this old bag and meet you on the other side of the swamp."

"But what about the weeping willow tears?" Abbie cried.

"You let me worry about that, Abbie. Go!"

Bub grabbed the tracking device and fumbled for the distress signal button. Inside the frog's backpack, Pteron began to panic. His body trembled and his legs pumped like tiny pistons, awaiting Epona's wrath. After several powerful kicks to Bub's back, the frog became agitated. "Knock it off, Ace. You're making it impossible for me to hit the distress signal." He jostled his pack up and down to send the dragonfly a clear message. Pteron crashed into Bub's flashlight. A powerful beam escaped and pointed directly into Epona's wicked eyes.

"AHHHHHH!!!" the bog lady shrieked, covering her hollow face with two bony hands.

"She's afraid of the light," Alex yelled. "Bub, don't send the distress signal. I think we've got this old girl cornered. You and Abbie grab your flashlights and aim them at her face." Alex yanked his flashlight from his pack as the others fumbled for their own. Within seconds, three strong beams of light found their target, and Epona released an ear-splitting wail. She shrunk into a shriveled ball and disappeared into the depths of the moss-laden swamp.

"It worked!" Bub yelled. He hopped up and down, waving his flashlight in the air.

"Hey! What is this, frog? A bull-riding contest?" Pteron clung tightly to Bub's flashlight. "Take it easy!"

The group, relieved by Epona's departure, broke into fits of laughter. Pteron wasn't amused. He quickly tested his wings and took off, heading for the nearest swamp exit.

"Hold on, Pteron," Alex said as he chased the departing insect. "Where do you think you're going?"

"We bumped into that wicked swamp lady and lived to tell about it," Pteron said. "That's about all the excitement I can take. It's time for this dragonfly to go home."

"Oh, no you don't. We didn't come all this way to quit at the first sign of trouble," Alex said. He snatched Pteron out of the air and glared into the dragonfly's agitated eyes. "Lead the way, Ace. We've got some weeping willow tears to collect."

Chapter Seven
In Search of Tears

"You *do* realize we have no guarantee these willows will weep," Pteron snapped at Alex, who held the dragonfly securely in his grip.

"Well, I guess we'll have to take our chances, won't we?" Alex responded. A confident smirk creased his lengthy snout. The irritable insect was difficult to deal with, but he was growing on the young alligator. "Just keep us headed in the right direction, Ace. We'll deal with whatever problems come our way, *when* they come our way."

"We should be approaching the….willow thicket…any minute…" Pteron grimaced, struggling to free himself from Alex's grasp. "It's on the very edge of the swamp, where the trees can get sunlight. Look, gator, if you would…argh…let me loose, I could fly ahead and check things out."

"Not a chance," Alex chuckled. "You'd be outta here in a flash if I let you go. Just keep those jumbo peepers of yours peeled and lead us to the willows."

Pteron, no match for Alex's determination, accepted his fate and pointed the little band east toward daylight.

As they approached the swamp's perimeter, Bub cried out, "Abbie! Alex! Look over there!" The outline of three large weeping willows appeared through the dense swamp mist. "We found them! They really do exist!"

Abbie glanced at Alex. Her eyes brightened as she splashed through the shallow waters toward the willows' graceful, drooping canopies. Alex, Pteron and Bub followed quietly behind.

"Wait. What's that noise?" Abbie asked. "It sounds like…is it snoring?"

"It's the willows," Pteron said. "They're sleeping. And they won't be too happy if we wake them. These particular trees are rumored to be very ill-tempered, which kind of explains the weeping…"

"We got it, Ace," Alex interrupted. "Since you know so much about these willows, maybe you should be the one to shake them out of their slumber."

"You're kidding, right?" Pteron replied. "You drag me all this way, almost serve me up as dinner to the bog lady, hold me in a vice-grip for the last hour, and now you want ME to save the day…again?"

Alex howled with laughter. "Refresh my memory, dragonfly; when exactly did you save the day?"

"Enough with the bickering, you two," Abbie said. "I'll do it." She pulled a rubber band from her wrist and tied back her long, golden hair.

"No, Abbie," Alex said. "It could be dangerous." He walked toward the salamander and, without thinking, released

Pteron. The startled dragonfly tumbled to the murky, swamp
floor. Angry and covered with mud, Pteron thrashed his
multiple legs in an attempt to shower the careless alligator with
swamp gunk but succeeded only in further covering himself.

"Abbie," Alex said. "We don't know how the willows will
react. I can't put you in a position where you might get hurt."

"Well now, gator, you didn't seem to be too worried about
my well-being," Pteron complained. Alex and Abbie ignored the
whining bug.

"Alex, I'm putting myself in this position," said Abbie.
"I'm a big girl. Don't treat my like a newborn."

Alex lowered his head and let out a loud sigh. "Alright,"
he said. "But I'll be right behind you."

"And so will I," Bub said.

"No. You're staying right here, Tadpole," Alex ordered.
"I mean it. Someone's gotta keep an eye on the dragonfly. He's
been trying to escape for hours."

"Alright," Bub said, disappointed. "Pteron and I will
stay behind."

"You better believe we will," Pteron said. He was
perched on Bub's backpack, vigorously shaking himself and
splattering mud in all directions.

"Watch it!" Bub shouted.

"Shhhh," Abbie whispered. "You two are going to upset
the willows. Now, cool it." She walked toward the thicket, and
Alex followed close behind. They reached the outer ring of
drooping limbs moments later. Sunlight speckled the earth
beneath the trees. Their long branches hung like streamers,

the tips occasionally touching the ground as they moved up and down with each slumbering snore.

Abbie ducked under the largest willow's broad canopy and approached its sturdy trunk. "Excuse me," she said in a soft voice.

The snoring continued.

Abbie spoke louder. "Excuse me, Mister Willow. Are you awake?"

Nothing.

"HELLO!" she screamed, banging her fist on the tree's trunk.

"Wha...who's there?" the willow howled, mouth agape. Spotting Abbie, it lashed out, waking the trees on either side. "What do you want? Get out of here! Out! Out! Out!"

"But...but, Mister Willow," Abbie said. She crouched near the tree's trunk. Alex ran to her side, dodging branches as they whipped through the air. Abbie tried again. "Please, stop swinging at us. We...we just have a small favor to ask."

"No favors!" the willow boomed. The trees were in full attack mode, coiling their slender limbs and slapping at the pesky creatures invading their space. Abbie and Alex ducked and rolled to avoid their stinging lashes.

"We just need a few measly tears!" Alex shouted. "We're trying to save our town. I promise, if you oblige us today, we'll never bother you again."

"Tears, tears, tears...everyone is always wanting our tears," the largest willow snarled. "Well, we're tired of it!" His pals on either side shook their great manes in agreement. Their oval eyes, almost hidden by countless leafy tendrils, showed no signs of shedding the magical antidote. They were bone dry.

"If you would just listen...HEY, PUT US DOWN!" Abbie and Alex were suddenly snatched off the ground by the grouchy willows, and despite protests, thrown clear of the thicket and into the mud at Bub's feet.

"Nice job, *Ace*," Pteron smirked as he flew just out of Alex's reach.

"Clam it, dragonfly," the gator grumbled. He regained his footing and plucked a wet reed from between his sharp teeth. He then grabbed Abbie's outstretched hand and pulled her to her feet.

"Are you hurt?"

"No, I'm fine." Abbie squeezed brackish water from her

long ponytail and straightened her grimy clothing.

"What now, Alex?" she cried. "Those cranky trees aren't going to willingly shed their tears." Her sadness troubled Alex, but he had no answers.

"Look folks, we did what we could; it just didn't work out," Pteron chimed in. "It's time to get out of this creepy swamp."

"That's it?" Bub asked. "We're quitting? Is that what we're doing, Alex?" The distressed frog looked to his idol for reassurance.

"We're in over our heads, Tadpole. Those selfish willows aren't going to budge. And without the tears, we don't have anything." Alex avoided the eyes of his disappointed friend. "It's time to go home…help out where we're most needed."

"Great idea! Let's get moving, folks!" said Pteron. His upbeat tone irked the others. "I'm worn out, so I'll need to hitch a ride in someone's pack. But I'd prefer it not be the young frog's. He's got that smelly onion in there. It irritates my eyes; makes 'em water like crazy."

"What did you say?" Alex asked, an idea forming in his mind.

"I said I don't want to ride in the frog's pack. You don't expect me to…"

"Pipe down for a minute, Ace, and let me think." Alex turned to Bub. "Tadpole, did you bring one of your onions to munch on?"

"Well, yeah. I forgot I even had it. Why?"

"Think about it," Alex said. "You love eating onions, but

what happens when you get those fumes in your eyes?"

Bub smiled. "I think I know where you're going with this, gator."

"Alex, you're right!" Abbie exclaimed. She ran to Bub and helped him pull off his pack. "The onion...we can use it to *make* the willows cry. No one said they had to be tears of sorrow." Abbie scooped up the little frog and wrapped him in a hearty embrace. "Oh Bub, I love you and your stupid onions!"

"Wait a minute," Pteron said. "We were supposed to be leaving this horrible place. I was going to sleep on my own pond tonight. I *am* going to sleep on my own pond tonight."

"It's dried up, Ace," Alex said. "There's no pond to go home to. Besides, you've got work to do. You're about to deliver an onion to some willows."

"I'd like to see you make that happen, gator."

Chapter Eight
Grumpy Willows

"Abbie and I will distract the willows while you fly the onion near their eyes," Alex told Pteron. He then turned to Bub. "Tadpole, you stand at the base of the trees and catch the tears. Use your thermos cap. When it's full and you're out of danger, we'll transfer the tears to a candy container I found in my backpack. Pteron, I'm going to cut into the onion, so put on your goggles. You'll need to protect your eyes from the fumes."

"I told you, gator, I'm done with these crazy quests. You can't force me to do this. I *refuse* to do this." Pteron stood erect on Bub's left shoulder, his many legs folded defiantly across his puffed-out chest.

"You just gear up, Ace," Alex replied, ignoring the dragonfly's protests. "Those willows aren't going to take this sitting down. You'll need to employ your best flying skills to avoid being knocked out of the air."

"Gator, are your ears working? I said I'm not going."

Alex approached the dragonfly. His steps were quick, and his face was determined. Mud splashed from beneath his feet into Pteron's gaping mouth.

"Alright! Alright!" Pteron screamed, realizing he'd pushed the gator too far. Alex scooped him up and tightened his fist around Pteron's shivering frame, causing the horrified insect to spit out a mouthful of mud. His large eyes bulged as he struggled to escape the alligator's grip.

"I've had enough of you, Ace," Alex spat through clenched teeth. "This isn't a game. This is our home we're trying to save, and you're going to help us!"

"Alex, don't hurt him," Abbie said. She cautiously placed a hand on her friend's shoulder. "He's just scared. We all are. But we mustn't quibble with each other. We've got to stick together."

Alex turned to face Abbie. Her soft voice had its usual calming effect, and his grip on the dragonfly loosened. Pteron let out a loud sigh and lay limp with relief in Alex's palm.

Abbie brushed aside a lock of hair and tucked it back into her hair band. "Pteron," she said. "We need you. You're quick and agile. Only you can get the onion near the willows' eyes."

Pteron sat up straight. "It is true," he said, fumbling to untangle his scarf from around a back leg. "I am quite skilled in flight. And I have the strength to carry many times my body weight."

"Then you see," Abbie concealed a victorious smile. "We simply can't do this without you. Will you help us, Pteron? Will you help us save our home?"

The dragonfly fluttered from Alex's open palm to the muddy ground. He arched his tiny back and marched to and fro in front of the trio. "It's clear to me that without my bravery, brawn and brains, we would never have made it this far," Pteron said.

A chuckle escaped Bub's lips. Abbie clamped her hand over his mouth and shot the frog a threatening glance.

Pteron eyed the two, paused briefly, and then continued. "I will, once again save you from your bumbling selves," he said. "Hand over the onion, alligator." The dragonfly reached for the onion with one set of legs, while pulling his goggles down with another.

"Hold your horses, Ace." Alex pulled a pocketknife from his jeans and placed the onion on a flat rock. "We need to cut into it. That will release the fumes and make the tears come quicker."

He cut the onion into quarters and held a section out to the now jittery insect. "Don't wimp out on us, Ace," Alex said. "This could be your shining moment."

"I'm not wimping out on anything," Pteron barked. He grabbed the onion piece from Alex and attempted to take off. It was heavier than expected, and he fluttered in crazy circles just above the ground, red-faced and huffing.

"Let me help you out," Alex said. He scooped up the struggling insect and tossed him high in the air. Pteron darted this way and that, plunging almost to the swamp floor before all four wings went into overdrive, and he was successfully in flight.

"Alright, let's get going," the dragonfly gasped, laboring to stay aloft. "I won't be able to carry this thing for long."

The group moved cautiously toward the willows, keeping cover behind moss-draped trees.

"It's got to be a surprise attack," Alex whispered. "We can't allow the willows time to react." He turned to Bub who was hopping alongside Abbie. "Bub, do you have the thermos cap?"

The frog nodded and held up the red lid.

"Good," Alex said. "Abbie and I are right behind you. The willows will be preoccupied with Pteron's buzzing around. Stay close to their trunks. They'll have trouble seeing you there. Keep an eye on Pteron and catch the tears when they begin to flow."

"Got it," Bub said. His excitement was boiling over.

"Stay calm, Tadpole," Alex cautioned. "We need to be smart about this. Once you've got the tears, we'll make a dash for the swamp's back entrance. It's over there," he pointed. "Right behind the willows."

"Quiet, fellows. There they are," Abbie whispered. The group hunkered behind a mass of reeds within a stone's throw of the willows. Overhead, Pteron was nearing exhaustion. It was time for action.

"Bub...Pteron," Alex said. "You know what you need to do. Are you ready?"

"I'm ready," Bub replied. Pteron nodded in agreement. The onion was growing heavier by the minute, and the dragonfly was beginning to lose his nerve.

"Okay, I'll count down from three," Alex said. "When I reach one, Bub, you and Pteron rush the willows. They haven't spotted us yet, and they seem to have settled down. You boys have a good chance of reaching them before you're noticed."

Through the trees, Abbie could see the sun sinking in a clear sky. They didn't have much time; just a few minutes before they lost what little light remained.

Alex began the countdown. "Three...two..." Bub was off and hopping, unable to wait any longer. Pteron flew behind him, strengthened by a surge of adrenaline pumping through his tiny veins.

"We're almost there," Bub yelled to Pteron. "Watch out for their branches. They'll be swatting at us from every angle. Get in close and head for their eyes. They won't be able to get to you there."

The wind whipped past Pteron's head as he gained speed. His legs lay tight against his body, his multiple wings a blur of motion. As the two zoomed toward the outer reach of the willows, they were spotted.

"What the..." the largest willow exclaimed. "Those scoundrels are back!" The tree began to wildly lash out with its hundreds of leafy tendrils. Pteron could hear them whistling through the air, but he continued on, heading directly for the eyes of the angry willow.

"Ouch! Watch it, willow," Pteron yelped as one of the branches nicked his side, throwing him temporarily off balance. He recovered quickly and was near his target when another tendril stung him. It was a direct hit; right in the jaw. Pteron flew backward, flipping end over end. Several hazy moments passed before he regained control and realized the onion was no longer in his grasp.

"Oh no," he yelled. "Bub, where are you? I dropped the onion!"

The willows, satisfied that the dragonfly was no longer a threat, set their sights on Bub.

"Bub, watch out!" Pteron screeched as the frog bent to pick up the onion. A serpent-like branch cut through the air, narrowly missing the agile amphibian.

"Over here!" Pteron shouted, attempting to distract the willows. He zoomed toward them with lightning speed. "Come and get me, you cowardly old grumps." The trees, stunned by the insect's taunting words, shifted their attention just long enough for Bub to retrieve the prized onion.

"I've got it," Bub yelled from below. "I'll toss it up to you, Pteron. Here it comes." Bub lobbed the onion toward the dragonfly who raced past flailing branches to snare it in mid air. Bub, amazed by Pteron's skillful acrobatics and newfound courage, readied the thermos cap and settled down to watch the dragonfly in action.

Pteron first concentrated on the center and largest willow, hovering inches from its trunk...just out of reach. The willow gasped as Pteron flapped his wings furiously and extended his two front legs, directing the powerful fumes into the tree's eyes.

"THIS is what will get me home," Pteron screamed. "Now, out with those blasted tears!" The willow's eyelids began to flutter as the fumes took effect.

"Get ready Bub," Pteron said. "Here they come!"

The excited frog took his position, and a flood of tears began to fall. The willow begged for relief, but the dragonfly ignored its pleas. Bub's thermos cap was half full before Pteron moved to the next tree.

"Over here, Bub," he shouted.

Bub again moved into position, and within seconds, the thermos cap was full. "We've got plenty," the frog called out. "Let's get out of here."

Pteron turned to the third willow and winked. "It's your lucky day, my friend. You get to keep your tears...for now." The grateful tree sighed and curled up in its branches as the others struggled to recover, their eyes continuing to water.

Pteron dropped the onion and flew toward Alex and Abbie's hideout. Bub followed close behind, careful not to lose any of the precious tears.

"You did it," Abbie cried. She grabbed Pteron who struggled to catch his breath. "You really are a hero."

"Let's not celebrate prematurely," Alex said. "We still need to seal up the tears and get out of here. Bub, give me the thermos cap. I'll transfer the tears to my container. Grab one of those wide leaves." He pointed to a patch of thick, green bushes.

"What do you need a leaf for?" Bub asked as he picked one and handed it to Alex.

"To create a funnel," the alligator explained. "We don't want to lose a single drop." Alex rolled up the large leaf and stuck the narrow end into the empty tube. He carefully poured the contents of the brimming thermos cap into the wide end of the leaf and snapped on the tube's plastic cap. They had their magic willow tears.

"Let's get out of here," Abbie said. "We're losing sunlight."

"You can ride with me, buddy." Bub plucked Pteron from Abbie's hand and placed him in his backpack. The exhausted dragonfly smiled, curled up in a tight ball, and fell into a deep slumber.

Chapter Nine
A Prelude to Perregrim

Sunset came quickly following the group's hasty exit from the swamp, giving them little time to find an adequate resting place for the night. Pteron was still asleep as they set up camp a mile downriver, in a grove of thirsty, lifeless trees. It was meager shelter, but it would have to do. They needed their sleep; tomorrow was a big day. They were paying Petros Perregrim a visit.

***

"Wake up, Pteron," Alex whispered to the slumbering dragonfly. "Dawn's breaking. We need to get moving."

Pteron opened a sleepy eye and glared at the alligator.

"Let's go, Ace," Alex pushed.

The dragonfly ignored the relentless reptile and fell back into a glorious dream...he was home, and his mother had just finished preparing his favorite dish, fried mosquito. The first juicy bite was on its way to his mouth when...

"Alright, we'll do this the hard way," Alex said, snatching

Pteron from Bub's fluffy sleeping bag. The dragonfly's mouth still watered at the thought of his mother's cooking, and his anger grew as he shook off the weariness and realized where he was.

"What's your rush, alligator," Pteron complained. "We've got all day to get home."

The dragonfly fluttered back to Bub's cozy sleeping bag and buried himself inside. He could use a few more hours of sleep.

Alex grabbed Pteron again. "We're not going home, you foolish bug. We're headed to Petros Perregrim's compound. Why in the world do you think we risked our lives gathering those willow tears?"

"I'm sorry...*WHO* risked their life?" Pteron challenged. "I don't remember a gator offering to carry any onions. What I remember..."

"Doesn't matter," Alex interrupted. "We have more work to do. So, shake off the sleep, and get yourself ready to go."

"Look, you brutish reptile, I think there's been a misunderstanding." A nervous laugh escaped Pteron's mouth as he struggled to break free. "*YOU* and your two buddies are more than welcome to go to that evil man's fortress, but my mission is complete. I got you the tears. What you do with them is your business."

Bub, now awake, rolled up his sleeping bag and chuckled at the bickering duo. He knew the dragonfly didn't stand a chance, but the stubborn little insect stood his ground.

"Now, why don't you folks get moving," Pteron

continued. "I think I'll stay and get some more shut-eye before I head home. It's been a real pleasure, Alex, but it's time for us to part company."

"Nice try, Ace, but we're not finished with you yet. In a matter of hours, we'll be staking out Perregrim's place. Once we locate the source of his poisonous sludge, you're going to fly over and drop in the willow tears. Got it?"

Pteron wriggled some more, but Alex's grip was tight. He shot a steely look at the amused alligator, whose victorious grin sent the dragonfly over the edge. Pteron reared his head back, opened his wide mouth, and bit into one of Alex's toes with surprising force.

"Hey!" Alex yelped in pain, causing him to release the dragonfly.

"Adios, gator," Pteron shouted as he promptly took flight and headed for the river. He had finally escaped.

"Hold on, friend," a soft voice purred. Abbie, who'd been walking near the river, yanked Pteron out of the air by his ever-present scarf. Her sad gaze held his attention as he dangled, waiting for her to speak.

"See this river," she said, gently placing the dragonfly in her palm. He was free to go, but he didn't move. "This is our lifeblood," Abbie continued. She seemed distracted, looking beyond Pteron. "Only a trickle remains; not enough to sustain life. And where we're headed - Perregrim's compound - the water is contaminated. Are you okay with that, Pteron? You live near the water; part of your support system is this very river. Don't you realize this threatens your family and home as well as ours?"

"I do, Abbie," Pteron said. "I just don't know why fixing it is my responsibility." His words were not harsh. He respected the lovely amphibian.

"It's not your responsibility *alone*," Abbie said. "It's *ours*...all of ours. We each have special skills. Yours is the ability to fly. It's very possible that Perregrim's sludge is manufactured with large pieces of equipment; equipment too tall and massive for the rest of us to scale. We need a partner that can reach those heights. Please join us on this mission, Pteron. I promise, if we make it out safely, you'll be free to go."

"What else is there," Pteron replied. "If the tears work and we clear up the river water, then we're done; we've achieved the objective. Of course I can go home."

Pteron hopped out of Abbie's palm to the dry ground below and flitted back and forth. Bub and Alex began to move in their direction, but Abbie held up her hand; stopping them from coming closer.

"Pollution is only half the battle," Abbie said. "Look at the river. We're upstream of Perregrim's waste. Here, the water is clear, but what do you see?"

Pteron stared at the wilted brush alongside the barely trickling stream.

"There's not much water flowing," he observed. "But there's nothing we can do about that. We've had almost no rainfall this year and even less snowmelt from Mt. Kirati. We can't bully Mother Nature, Abbie."

Abbie shimmied down the riverbank to the water's edge.

Pteron followed. "You're right," she said. "The spring rains have been light. But this…" Abbie pointed to the nearly dry riverbed. "…this is not solely caused by a decrease in rainfall and snowmelt. There's something else going on." Abbie paused for a moment. "It is our hope that Pansophigus, the eagle at the top of Mt. Kirati, can tell us what it is."

Alex and Bub moved closer, straining to hear the conversation between Abbie and Pteron.

"We need to wrap this up," Alex cautiously interrupted. "If we hang around here much longer, we're going to lose the whole day."

He joined Abbie and Pteron in the riverbed. "Before we can tackle these other issues, we need to take care of Perregrim. Dragonfly or not, we've got to get moving."

Abbie turned to face Pteron. The dragonfly lingered on a large rock normally covered with rushing river water. "You know, Pteron, you're right. We've held you against your will long enough," Abbie said. "You're free to go."

"Rubbish," Pteron said, surprising the others…and himself. "You can't sneak into Perregrim's compound without me. I'm the brains behind this operation." Alex and Bub grinned as the pompous dragonfly opened his tiny pack and pulled out a wrinkled map of the area. "Now, let's start formulating a plan."

Chapter Ten
Storming the Compound

Perregrim's compound loomed a half mile downriver, but the stench of his trash heap army and poisonous sludge were already overwhelming.

"Whew, this is awful," Abbie said. She pulled a powder blue handkerchief from her backpack and placed it over her snout. "What *is* that smell?"

"It's Perregrim's smelly guards," Pteron replied. He hovered above the group, eyes red and teary from the foul odor. The dragonfly yanked down his goggles to dull the pain. "His soldiers aren't like anything I've ever seen before; it's as if they're made of garbage or something. They have all kinds of rotting, nasty stuff dripping off their sludgy..."

"Alright, enough," Alex interrupted. "We get the picture." He turned to the group. "Bub, get a handkerchief and cover your nose like Abbie. You, too, Pteron." Pteron obeyed by wrapping his aviator scarf tightly around his nose and mouth. Alex stared at the dragonfly in disbelief. "Hey, Ace," he chuckled. "You *do* need to breathe. You might consider uncovering your mouth. You'll serve us better alive."

Pteron lifted the scarf and let out a loud gasp. Alex shook his head and turned toward Perregrim's forbidding compound. "Pteron, get your map back out. We need to review our plan of attack."

The dragonfly perched himself on Bub's shoulder. "Hey, frod," he said. With his nose tightly wrapped, Pteron spoke as if suffering from a horrible head cold. Bub snickered at the insect.

"Help a dradonfly oud, would ya?" Pteron continued. "Open my pack and drab dat map. Id's on top."

Bub plucked Pteron from his shoulder and dug into the insect's tiny bag. He pulled out the wrinkled paper and spread it out on the dry ground.

"Here's where we are," Abbie said, pointing at the map. "Now, look downriver. See those three large stones about a quarter mile from here, near the river bend?"

The others looked off in the distance. The impressive structures rose high into the sky.

"Wow," Bub said. "That must be Stonesgate. Mrs. Wainscott said the stones were transported here by humans over three thousand years ago."

"That's right," Abbie replied. "And like the map indicates, it's just below Perregrim's compound. If we head southwest, we'll end up in front of the fortress. Pteron...Bub...stay behind me and Alex. Once we get moving, there can't be any talking; not a peep from you two. Perregrim's army will be on the lookout for unwelcome visitors."

Alex pointed out the compound's location on the map.

"We need to approach the building from the backside," he said.

"Why?" asked Bub.

"Because Perregrim's soldiers are lined up in the front." Alex wiped his brow and adjusted his shirt. He felt responsible for the group's safety. "Follow me," he said. "The map shows a large shed in back. If it's clear of soldiers, we'll use it for cover."

Alex turned to Pteron, again perched on Bub's shoulder. "Alright, Ace," he said. "This is where you come in. The soldiers won't pay much attention to a dragonfly buzzing around, so you're our eyes and ears. We need you to find a way into the compound and then pinpoint where Perregrim is brewing his mind-control substance. Once you've located the safest route, come back out, and we'll all go in together."

"Is dat *ALL* you'd lide me to do, dator," Pteron grumbled.

"That's it, Ace," Alex replied. "Now quit your whining and get ready."

"I'm confused, Alex," said Abbie. "Why doesn't Pteron fly in with the tears and take care of the problem on his first trip? Why do we all need to put ourselves in danger?"

Abbie's comment caused Pteron to break into a violent shaking fit. To calm the trembling insect, Bub hid him in his palm.

"It's not that simple, Abbie," said Alex. "A dragonfly carrying a container full of tears will arouse suspicion. We need to identify an exact location before we attack. And Pteron shouldn't have to face this alone. Perregrim's strongest guards will be protecting the potion. They won't go down easy."

"Did I already mention that I'm not real trazy about dis

plan." Pteron peeked from between Bub's fingers. His eyes expanded to the size of his goggles.

"We realize that," said Alex. "But we simply don't have a choice, Pteron. You're our only hope of going in unnoticed."

Pteron pulled his scarf down to better articulate his words. "Well, then, let's get this over with," he said, exhaling loudly. "The waiting is driving me nuts."

"Alright," Alex said. "Let's get moving. Pteron, ride in Bub's backpack. You'll need all the energy you can muster. And remember, no talking until we reach the shed."

***

Several minutes passed before Perregrim's terrifying fortress came into view. The horrible odor of his army and the pollutants that surrounded them were almost unbearable.

"I'm gonna pass out," Pteron squealed. His wings began to flutter inside Bub's pack.

"Put your scarf back on, bug," Alex replied.

The dragonfly glared at the annoyed alligator before pulling the scarf over his nose. Like it or not, the cranky gator was right. He wouldn't accomplish anything with tear-soaked eyes and a churning stomach.

Abbie and Bub held handkerchiefs up to their faces and took short, quick breaths to combat their own nausea. Alex continued to 'tough it out' but was beginning to falter.

"We'll stay behind that strip of trees," Alex whispered, pointing to a dark thicket. "It'll lead us directly to the shed."

The trees' bare branches provided little protection from peering eyes, but it would have to do. They scurried from one grove to the next, careful to avoid the brittle leaves that littered the earth. The slightest noise could blow their cover.

As expected, a large, rotting wooden shed was located near the compound's back entrance. A clearing stood between the group and the coverage that the building provided.

"There's a guard patrolling near the shed," Alex whispered, halting the group.

"That ain't good," Bub croaked.

"He's probably on a schedule," Alex continued. "We'll wait here until he comes back around." The group sat silent as Alex kept his eye on the creature's route, occasionally glancing at his watch.

"Look, Alex," Abbie whispered. "He's already back."

The guard slithered within a few feet of the shed and scanned the area before turning back in the other direction. From the shadows, Alex winced at the disgusting creature's odor. The alligator could stand the smell no longer. He reached into his backpack, pulled out a handkerchief and placed it over his flaring nostrils.

"Alright," Alex said, glancing at his watch one last time. "It looks like he passes this way about every two minutes. That gives us plenty of time to run from the shed to the fortress once Pteron returns."

Alex plucked the dragonfly from the safety of Bub's backpack. "Are you ready, little buddy?"

Pteron nodded. He attempted to speak, but paralyzing

fear had stolen his voice.

"You'll be just fine," Abbie whispered to Pteron. She smiled and secured the tiny aviator scarf around his nose.

"Time to get going, Ace," Alex grunted. "Stay out of sight as best you can and be safe. We'll be waiting for you behind the shed."

The dragonfly hovered above the group and saluted them with the flick of a front leg. He then winged high into the cloudless sky to avoid the roaming eyes of Perregrim's troops and to gain a bird's-eye view of the area. Far below, Alex and the rest of the group strained to see the tiny insect.

"What's he doing? He's flying too high!" Abbie cried. "Why isn't he going inside?"

"Give him a little time," said Alex. "He's getting a lay of the land; finding a suitable entrance. We'll need that information when it's time for us to go in."

Pteron circled several times before spotting an open door. A steady stream of Perregrim's soldiers weaved into the cold, frightening compound, leaving trails of soupy sludge in their wake. He scanned the area once again, searching for a safer access point but found none.

"Good grief, I'll have to fly past those stinky soldiers to get inside. I'd better build up some major speed."

The dragonfly took a deep breath, pointed his head down and began his descent. His scarf fluttered wildly as he raced toward the compound, and without warning, it flipped over his goggles. *Everything went black.* Pteron flailed his legs in an attempt to pull the scarf away from his eyes, but was unable to grab hold of it in his downward spiral. From their hiding place, Pteron's friends watched in horror as the dragonfly plummeted toward earth.

"What's happening," Bub howled, panicked by Pteron's erratic dive. "Something's wrong. We've got to help him!"

"Keep your voice down," Abbie whispered. "We're going to be spotted if you…"

We've got to get over to that shed," Alex interrupted. "That's where Pteron will be looking for us." He checked the area for the patrolling guard. "I don't see that trash heap soldier. Let's make a run for it."

The trio tore across the clearing and, within seconds, arrived safely behind the ramshackle shed. Bub hopped nervously back and forth, searching for any sign of his dragonfly pal.

"Keep still, Bub," Abbie insisted. "Pteron is more than capable of taking care of himself. Odds are he's already in there scoping things out."

***

With only seconds to spare, Pteron grabbed hold of his scarf and yanked it away from his eyes.

"AHHHHHHH," he yelped, taking a hard right, narrowly missing one of the slimy soldiers. His scream startled the creature who instinctively swatted at the insect. But the dragonfly was too quick. He was through the door and inside the compound before the beast could stop him.

Pteron spotted a ledge just inside the entrance and perched briefly to catch his breath. The air was rancid and reeked of rotting trash. He pulled the tangled scarf over his nose to dull the stench.

"How did I get myself into this?" he gasped, wiping his sweaty brow and scanning the room with his bulbous eyes. The inside of the fortress was as dark and menacing as the outside. Its damp, stone walls supported high-beamed ceilings and broken light fixtures teetered on rusty chains, providing no light for the cavernous room. A lone sunbeam pierced the darkness from a small, barred window high on the facing wall. It revealed a filthy floor covered with slimy residue.

"Now that's just gross," Pteron muttered. "Must be left behind by all these putrid soldiers."

The dragonfly's instincts told him to follow the crowd, but his wildly thumping heart and rational mind pleaded with him to turn around and leave the unforgiving prison.

"Keep the line moving!" a mechanical voice demanded.

Pteron searched for the source of the distant voice in the dim light.

"Drink from the full ladle handed to you, and then get out!" it again boomed.

"What in the world is going on," Pteron thought. "Focus! Just find what you're here to find, and then hightail it out of this creepy place."

Pteron's heart pounded against his chest and all six knees knocked together so violently he feared the noise would give him away. "Shake it off. Shake it off. You're a flying ace...a hero. You can do this!"

The insect shook his head back and forth to clear the fear from his mind, and then zeroed in on the soldiers' shadowy movements. Their muddy, dripping bodies seemed almost fluid, as if they were in a state of constant change.   But most disturbing were the ghastly looks on their hollow faces. Mouths wide open, they emitted deep guttural sounds, like an animal howling in pain.

"It's time to make a move," he said, adjusting his goggles and pulling in a deep, steadying breath. "If these boys get hold of me, I might be the one wailing in pain. I've got to do this now, or I may lose my nerve."

Pteron hopped off the high ledge, took flight, and successfully weaved through several soldiers before entering a dark passageway. The creatures inside were not so forgiving. Upon hearing Pteron's wings buzzing past them, they blindly swung their arms in the air, spraying hundreds of droplets of putrid, liquid trash throughout the gloomy hall.   In the darkness, Pteron could hear the sludge as it splashed against the stone walls. He sped up, hoping for a hasty exit, or at least some sign of light.

Flying near the passageway's ceiling, Pteron could avoid the outstretched arms of the creatures below.   But as the hallway began to curve to the right, a droplet of scalding goop hit one of Pteron's boots. The dragonfly shook his foot as the burning liquid ate through the sturdy leather.

＊

"He's been in there too long," Bub whispered. "Something's happened. I can feel it."

"Quiet, Bub," said Alex. "The guard is coming back around."

"But what about Pteron?"

"Shhhhhh," Alex hissed.

The approaching guard paused at the unfamiliar noise. Alex, Abbie and Bub held their breath as the creature searched the landscape. Several tense moments passed before the soldier turned in the other direction and continued its patrol, leaving a trail of dead grass in its wake.

"What did I tell you, Bub," Alex said through gritted teeth. "You're going to blow our cover if you don't keep quiet."

"I'm just worried about Pteron."

"We all are," Alex said. "But we have got to be patient. If he made it inside, he'll need time to stake out the area and find a safe entry and exit for the rest of us. If he doesn't come out in the next few minutes, we'll go in after him."

***

Pteron worked to untie his scalding boot as he raced through the cramped passageway. He felt the fiery substance nip at his toes as the leather disintegrated.

"Ow! Ow!" he shrieked. The sullen soldiers squinted to find the source of the disturbance. In the distance, a faint light came into view. Pteron untied the last lace and shed his mangled boot, sending it hurling toward the creatures below.

He picked up speed to avoid their wrath.

A room at the end of the narrow hallway came into view, and the approaching light allowed the dragonfly to more clearly see the path in front of him. In the distance, he could hear the mechanical voices.

"Move it! Move it!" they yelled. "Take your drink, pass the ladle to the soldier behind you, and head back to your guard posts!"

Pteron flew higher as the light revealed the passageway's ceiling. "Gotta stay out of reach," he muttered. The entrance to the room was just ahead, and he slowed down to gain control. The soldiers below slithered forward, indifferent to the screaming voices ahead.

On each side of the room's entrance, small ledges held burning candles. Their flickering flames cast grotesque shadows on the damp walls. Hot wax dripped to the floor as the drones below steadily moved forward. Pteron flew to one of the ledges and perched briefly, lifting his now-exposed foot to avoid the burning wax. He strained his neck to see into the cavernous room on the other side of the doorway. What he witnessed was unimaginable.

In the center of the chaotic room stood a monstrous circular vat. Its contents were thick and brown and bubbling over. The room's eerie light seemed to emanate from the floor, as if the earth below was glowing from some hidden energy source. Pteron swallowed hard. He had found Perrergrim's mind-control potion.

"Stay calm," he muttered, but his tiny voice trembled

with fear. "This is no big deal. Just pretend you're at home hovering over a pot of mom's famous mosquito stew."

The thought calmed Pteron, and he scanned the ceiling for another landing place. It was important he get a full view of the room and the creatures within it. Several dark, wood beams crossed the length of the space; a perfect vantage point for the dragonfly. He jumped from his waxy perch and flew along the perimeter of the cavernous room, dodging intricate spider webs and their eight-legged inhabitants. Below, the percolating mind-control substance spilled onto several of Perregrim's slimy minions, who screamed in pain. A mechanical arm hovered above the boiling pot, stirring its contents, while several sturdy robots barked orders at the guards below.

Now safely on the central beam, Pteron watched as one of the ill-tempered robots climbed a ladder to the edge of the bubbling cauldron. He dipped a ladle into the red-hot contents and passed it to his co-worker several rungs below, who in turn, passed it to a third robot located on the ground.

"Guzzle it down and get back to your post," the droid ordered, thrusting the overflowing ladle in the face of the next trash heap in line.

The creature took the ladle, drank its fill, and instantly began to run in circles, splashing muddy goop on the weary soldiers nearby.

"Out!" the robot yelled. The soldier obeyed. It ran, arms waving, through the main entrance and to its guard post in front of Perregrim's fortress.

"Something in the brew is reviving those nasty minions," Pteron whispered. "But where is the pollution coming from?" The dragonfly searched the area and spotted a large hose extending from the bottom of the vat, through the front wall, to the outside. "There it is!" he squealed. "That's how the poisonous sludge gets to the river."

Pteron's eyes swept the room once more, looking for additional robots. There were none. "Not bad odds," he said. "We can easily overpower these three boys. But I've *got* to find a safer entry point. The others will be spotted immediately if they come in the same way I did."

As Pteron sought another option, a heavy door flew open, slamming against the stone wall. The startled dragonfly shot straight up, hit his head on the hard ceiling, and fell back to the thick beam.

Heavy footsteps pounded the stone floor. "WHAT'S TAKING SO LONG IN HERE!" a terrifying voice boomed. "I ONLY HAVE HALF AN ARMY OUTSIDE!"

The line of dripping soldiers cowered as Petros Perregrim stomped over to a petrified robot and grabbed its metal head. He lifted the mechanical being off the floor and glared into its red, pinhole eyes. "I told you to have *all* the soldiers through here by mid morning," he sneered. "You're hours behind schedule. What's your excuse today?"

The robot had no response. A full ladle dropped from its hand and fell to the floor, splashing more burning liquid onto the frightened soldiers below.

"YOU HAVE NOTHING TO SAY?" Perregrim screamed.

His face turned bright red, and his rim of wild hair stood on end.

The robot shook its head. Its insides whirred with fear.

"You worthless pile of junk," Perregrim growled. "I'm done with you."

The robot's red pupils flared as Perregrim swung its metal body high above the floor, tossing it into the bubbling cauldron. A small explosion erupted as the droid became yet another ingredient in the dreadful stew.

"How about you other buckets of bolts!" he boomed. "Would you like to suffer the same fate?"

The two remaining robots shook their heads, wailing, "No sir, no sir. We'll push the guards through right away."

"You better believe you will," Perregrim replied. "These slimy creatures are my guinea pigs. My mind-control potion has got to be perfect. It can't continue to wear off this fast. How am I to control the planet with something that won't last?"

Perregrim glared at the quaking robots. A chewed-up cigar dangled from his fat lips and his yellow teeth ground together in frustration.

"Where's the chemist?" he screamed. "He's got work to do. Go get him...NOW!"

Perregrim turned to leave, tossing several soldiers aside and flicking his mangled cigar at the robots. "I'll be back in an hour," he said. "If these vile creatures aren't back at their posts, and if that chemist isn't hard at work, you two dimwits will be joining your friend."

Pteron rubbed his throbbing head and watched in terror

as the lumbering giant yanked open the door, sending it slamming once more against the cold, stone walls.

"That man is unbelievable," he whispered. "If we don't do something quick, his evil plan just might work."

Below, the two remaining robots tossed ladles back and forth at a feverish pace. They forced the revolting concoction down the throats of confused soldiers and quickly sent them along.

In the opposite corner of the room, a pile of crumbling stones caught Pteron's eye. Several rats scurried inside through a small opening. They carried materials to an elaborate nest near the warmth of the giant vat. The dragonfly flew down for closer inspection. "This could work. It's a good distance from the vat, far enough to come and go unnoticed. And if we knock a few more stones loose, the others should be able to squeeze through." Excited by his discovery, Pteron flew through the existing hole to the shed that concealed his friends.

***

"You're back!" Bub howled, unable to contain his excitement. Abbie and Alex warned him to keep quiet, but their own joy at Pteron's return was difficult to mask.

"Welcome back, Ace. We were getting worried," Alex said. He pulled out some bottled water, uncapped it, and tilted it forward for the insect to drink. "Drink up, and then tell us everything you know. But talk low. The guard will be coming around soon."

"Let a guy catch his breath, will ya," Pteron replied, guzzling the precious water. "There's a lot to tell and even more to accomplish."

Pteron settled on Bub's shoulder and removed his backpack. While Perregrim's guard made his round near the shed, the dragonfly took a moment to relax. Once the creature passed, Pteron replayed his frightening experiences and provided the group with a detailed description of the compound's layout. The others were stunned by what he had seen...and by Perregrim's evil plan.

"Pteron, you did a wonderful job," Abbie whispered. "It sounds like we need to get in there right away. Let's hope these tears do the trick."

"Yeah, they better," the weary dragonfly said, pulling on his backpack. "Follow me. We'll slip through the wall after the guard comes back around."

***

Pteron's assumption was correct. Alex easily removed additional stones from the wall, creating an opening large enough for the team to slip through. They shimmied in unnoticed with plenty of time to spare.

Pteron's description of the cavernous room had been vivid, but nothing could have prepared them for the reality of seeing it first-hand.

Alex held up his hand. "Listen up, folks," he whispered. "I know this is overwhelming, but we've got to stay focused.

Let's post ourselves at different spots around the room. Pteron needs our protection while he's delivering those tears. Whatever happens, we have to make sure he's able to do his job."

Outside, Perregrim's guard glimpsed a rat scurrying toward the back corner of the building and decided to follow the varmint. As he approached the compound wall, he noticed a gaping hole.

"Those rocks are too heavy for a rat to move," the disgusting creature gurgled. "I'd better take a closer look."

He stuck his head through the opening and bumped right into Bub's back. The frog leapt forward, stung by the dripping guard's sludge. Abbie and Alex turned toward the commotion and found themselves face to face with one of Perregrim's own.

"RUN!" Alex yelled. The three scattered in different directions while Pteron flew toward the ceiling, barely avoiding the grasp of the angry soldier.

"INTRUDERS! WE HAVE INTRUDERS!" the goon shouted.

The robots and remaining guards turned toward the screaming soldier.

"Abbie!" Alex yelled. "The tears are in the plastic tube in your pack. Get them to Pteron!"

Abbie hid behind a massive control unit and removed her backpack. Her hands shook as she fumbled with the zipper.

"Up here!" Pteron called out from above. "Toss the bottle up here!"

Abbie took a deep breath and tried the zipper again. A robot was headed in her direction, and he was closing in fast.

"Hurry, Abbie! Hurry!" Pteron squealed.

The salamander tugged at the zipper with all her strength until it finally gave way. She grabbed the tube of tears, tossed it in the air, and ran for the exit. The dragonfly took a sharp dive and caught the precious cargo just inches above the filthy floor. He swooped back up and headed for the bubbling vat.

Below, the robot nipped at Abbie's heels as she dashed for the hole in the crumbling wall. She was halfway through the opening when the robot clamped onto her ankle, pulling her back inside. Its laser-red eyes bore into the salamander. "You're coming with me, intruder," it whirred. "We're going to see the boss."

"Not today, bot!" Alex roared as he jumped the machine from behind and knocked him to the floor.

"Run, Abbie! Find Pteron! Make sure he drops the tears in the potion." Alex opened a panel on the robot's back and yanked several wires loose. The machine immediately ground to a halt and slumped over.

"Come with me," Abbie pleaded. "We need to find Bub, too. Have you seen him?"

"He was supposed to be watching over Pteron," Alex said.

"We've got to find them, Alex," Abbie cried. "I saw another robot, and there were dozens of Perregrim's grimy soldiers near that boiling pot."

The two ran toward the large vat in search of their friends, but found nothing.

"Come this way, Abbie," Alex said. "There's a ladder leading to the rim."

As they rounded the corner, they ran smack into Bub. But he wasn't alone.

"Well, well...look who we have here," Petros Perregrim growled. "To what do I owe the pleasure?" Cigar smoke swirled above his head, and an evil grin curled his lips. He held Bub in his massive grip.

"You let him go!" Alex yelled. "Or else I'll..."

"Or else you'll what, you yellow-bellied reptile!" Perregrim howled with laughter and turned toward the ladder. He grabbed the top rung, effortlessly climbed to the vat's rim, and dangled a frightened Bub over the boiling brew. "Looks like it's time for your little green buddy to say goodbye."

"We know what you're up to, Perregrim," Bub bravely croaked. "And we're not going to let you get away with it."

Perregrim's laughter again filled the steamy room. "I'd like to see you try," he bellowed. "You're in a pretty rocky position to be making such a bold statement, frog."

Out of the corner of his eye, Bub caught a glimpse of Pteron flying over the bubbling pot. "Quick, Pteron!" he cried. "Sprinkle in the tears...now!"

Perregrim immediately turned his attention to the dragonfly.

"Oh, no you don't," he screamed, tossing Bub, as luck would have it, into Alex's arms below. "I'm not going to let some measly insect ruin everything I've worked for!"

Perregrim clung to the ladder, swatting at Pteron with his thick arms. The dragonfly hovered just out of reach and carefully pulled the stopper out of the tube full of tears.

"You won't get away with this!" Perregrim shrieked. He lunged at Pteron, but the dragonfly escaped his grasp, causing the irate man to lose his balance. Perregrim teetered over the boiling cauldron, wildly flailing his arms. His face registered a look of terror. The crew below ran for cover just as their evil foe fell over the edge. A huge burst of steam billowed up and burning liquid splashed onto the ground, narrowly missing Abbie, Bub and Alex. Petros Perregrim was gone...swallowed by his own magic potion.

The group stood silent, hands over their mouths, until Alex snapped them out of their daze. "Sprinkle the tears, Pteron, NOW!"

Pteron crisscrossed the pot's surface several times, scattering a portion of the tears. A loud hissing noise followed, and a cloud of steam engulfed the room. As it cleared, Pteron let out a triumphant yell. "YAHOO!"

"What happened?" Alex called from below. "What do you see?"

"I see nothing," Pteron replied. "Absolutely nothing. It's all gone. The potion...the sludge...everything. It's all gone!"

Pteron flew in tight circles above the empty vat, celebrating their victory. Tears from the still-open tube dribbled onto Perregrim's grimy soldiers, huddled in a line near the huge cauldron.

"Look, Abbie!" Bub hopped about wildly, pointing at the once grungy soldiers. "There's a rabbit...and a field mouse! The tears are transforming the guards!"

"And a momma deer and her fawn," Abbie cried. "Oh, my! Perregrim must have been holding them captive with his potion. His soldiers...they're all woodland creatures."

"That explains the disappearance of all the wildlife," said Alex. "Pteron, come down here and bring me the tears. Be careful not to spill anymore."

The dragonfly fluttered down and landed on Bub's shoulder. Alex carefully took hold of the plastic tube and held it up to the light. "I don't think we have enough for all the soldiers," he said. "We've got to do something."

Pteron's eyes grew large. "I'm not going back to that swamp, gator," he replied.

"You won't need to," said a graceful deer as it strolled toward the group. "Perregrim had us constantly drinking his potion to keep it from wearing off. Every day, day after day, we had to file through this room. By tomorrow morning, our last dose should begin to wear off, and we'll be back to our original selves. We may all need a good bath, but we'll be free to return to our homes." The doe dropped her head for a moment. When she again looked up, a flood of tears fell from her soft brown eyes. "We're so thankful for what you've done."

"You and the others have been through so much," Abbie said. "We're just glad we could help." The doe nodded her head in appreciation and trotted away, grateful to be free.

"Follow me outside," Abbie said to Pteron. "Drop the

tears on the other soldiers until you run out. Alex…Bub, let's check the river; make sure there's no more sludge polluting it." The group paraded through the heavy wooden door and moved through the confused crowd of soldiers to the river.

"Perregrim is gone," Pteron yelled from above. "You're all free! I'll sprinkle as many of you as I can with the remaining willow tears. To the rest of you, don't worry. You, too, will be back to normal when the potion wears off. You can then find your family members and return to your homes."

Alex tossed the tears to Pteron, and the dragonfly began to shower them on the large group of soldiers huddled below. Within seconds, they morphed into the woodland creatures they had once been.

Beaming, Abbie, Alex and Bub headed for the river. A group of grateful animals followed close behind.

Abbie stood on the riverbank and smiled. "We did it," she said. "The sludge is gone. There's not a drop flowing from the pipe."

"But the water is still low," Bub remarked. "How will we survive without it?"

"That's why we have to continue on, Bub," Abbie said. "Our job isn't done. We've still got to meet with Pansophigus at the top of Mt. Kirati. He'll know what to do." She put an arm around her friend and pulled him close. "We've accomplished a lot, buddy. But without a sufficient water supply, it doesn't mean a thing."

"Then let's get going," Alex said. "We don't have much time."

Chapter Eleven
Bradley's Barrier

"We're out of tears," Pteron yelled from above. "I sprinkled most of the soldiers, and the others are satisfied to wait until the potion wears off."

"Good job, Pteron," said Abbie. At her side, Bub stared at the ground, aimlessly kicking a pile of dry river sand. It was time to tell his dragonfly friend goodbye, and the thought of it upset him terribly.

"Are you sure he can't stay with us, Abbie?"

"Bub, we've been holding Pteron against his will far too long. It's time to let him do as he wishes."

"But..."

"No but's, Tadpole. We need to let him go home."

Bub turned away and wiped a tear from his cheek. Abbie pulled the glum little frog close and hugged him tightly. "We'll see Pteron again," she assured him. "When the water is clear and the river is full, we'll see him again."

"But what if that never happens?"

"We can't think that way," said Abbie. "Now, c'mon, let's say our goodbyes. We need to get moving. There's not much time left to get to Pansophigus."

Bub spied the dragonfly in the distance. "Hey, buddy," he yelled. "Can you join us for a minute?"

Pteron dove toward Bub and landed on his shoulder.

"What's up, pal?" he asked.

"It's time for us to go," Bub replied. "We're headed for Mt. Kirati. It's crucial that we get as close as possible before nightfall."

Bub placed Pteron in his palm and looked into the dragonfly's large, expressive eyes. "So, I guess this is goodbye."

"What!" Pteron screeched. "You drag me all this way, and then drop me like a hot rock?" The dragonfly turned his head, unable to look his friend in the eye.

"No, of course not," Bub said. "I would love for you to join us, Pteron. Abbie just thought that…"

"Now hold on a minute, Bub," Abbie interrupted. She gingerly plucked the dragonfly from Bub's palm.

"Pteron, we've forced you to come all this way, placed you in dangerous situations, and refused to let you return home. Well, now's your chance. Are you saying you don't want to take it?"

Bub held his breath as he awaited the insect's response.

"You're right, of course," Pteron said. "I do want to go home, but it also appears that you want me out of your hair."

"No, Pteron," Abbie replied. "That's not true. It's just that…"

"Hey, I get it," Pteron whined. "I'm of no use to you anymore."

"Pteron, please." Abbie tried to reason with the dragonfly, but he abruptly took flight.

"Take care, frog." Pteron pulled off his aviator scarf and tossed it to Bub. "Keep this for good luck."

"That scarf almost cooked your goose earlier today," Alex interjected. "I'm not sure Bub needs that kind of luck."

"Be quiet, Alex!" Bub cried. He tied the scarf around his wrist, waved as Pteron sped away, then turned and stomped off in the direction of Mt. Kirati.

"Bub!" Abbie shouted.

"Let him have his space," said Alex. "He'll calm down by the end of the day."

***

Abbie kept Bub in sight as they moved toward the mountain. The sun was sinking fast behind the great peak, chilling the air. It was time to find a campsite and settle in for the night.

Abbie pulled a fluffy pink parka from her backpack and wrapped it tightly around her shivering shoulders.

"It's getting late, Alex," she said, exhausted by the day's long hike. "Let's catch up to Bub and find a safe place to camp."

"One more mile," Alex pushed. "If we can do that, we'll be in a better position to climb all the way up Mt. Kirati tomorrow."

Abbie shook her weary head but continued walking. The two stayed near the river channel, which sluggishly trickled with clean, clear water.

"Something is still restricting the river's flow," Abbie observed. "If it wasn't Perregrim, then who or what could it be?"

"I think Bub may have found the answer to your question," Alex replied. "Look upstream."

Abbie could just make out Bub, who was hopping up and down, pointing to a large pile of wood. The excited frog raced back toward Abbie and Alex. "I found it!"

Bub's labored breathing shot quick bursts of billowy fog into the cold air.

"Up ahead...I found what's blocking the river."

"Well, what is it?" Abbie asked.

"Follow me," Bub said as he hopped upstream toward his discovery. "I'll show you!"

Abbie gasped as the trio approached a massive structure spanning the width of the river.

"It looks like a beaver dam," Alex said, a puzzled look on his face. "But beavers build dams in streams and lakes, not across rivers."

From beneath the mound of limbs, stone and mud, a stout brown creature emerged.

"It is a beaver dam," said Alex, spotting the plump rodent.

The beaver protectively slapped his flat black tail on the sticks and mud beneath him, packing the material even tighter.

"Ain't a drop of water in the streams, alligator," the flannel-clad beaver barked. He jerked the flaps of his plaid

wool hat over a pair of tiny ears. "There wasn't more than a bucket of rain and snow this past winter. No rain or snow melt means no water in the streams. My family and I didn't have a choice. We had to head for the river."

"Hey, pal, don't you realize there are whole towns downstream that rely on this river water?" Alex growled. "You've jammed it up so bad, there's barely a trickle left for the rest of us."

"I can't worry about anyone else," the beaver replied, then turned to nibble on a tree trunk near the riverbank. "I've got a wife and kits counting on me to keep 'em safe. Besides, that polluted water downstream ain't worth drinking anyway."

"We've taken care of that, you selfish, oversized rat," Alex barked.

"Alex!" Abbie hissed. "Insults aren't going to get us anywhere. We've got to convince this stubborn creature to cooperate and take down his dam, so *stay calm*!"

"Bradley," a soft voice called from a nearby tree grove. "Who are you speaking with?"

"You critters need to vamoose," said the beaver. "I don't want you upsetting my wife and kits. They've been through enough this year."

"So the name's Bradley?" Abbie asked.

The beaver reluctantly nodded.

"My friend meant no offense," she continued. "But our families have had a bad year, too. If you would just listen to our story, I think you'll understand the importance of removing the dam and releasing the water behind it."

"Can't do it, missy," Bradley replied. "I can't destroy the only home we have; not until I see water flowing again in those mountain streams."

"Maybe we should hear them out, honey." Bradley's wife appeared at the river's edge, followed by three playful youngsters, all miniature versions of their father. "Boys, go inside. I'll be along shortly to feed you."

The tiny beavers raced along the bank and dove into the river's shallow, frigid water. They swam under the dam and through an underwater entrance, resurfacing inside the family's spacious, dome-shaped lodge.

"Ma'am..." Abbie began.

"Please, sweetheart, call me Brenda."

"Okay...Brenda," Abbie said. "Our beautiful home, Gaea, many miles downstream, is little more than a dry mud hole today. As we speak, our families are packing up to leave." Abbie walked to Alex and Bub and grabbed both of their hands. "My friends and I are headed to Mt. Kirati's summit. We're desperate for solutions."

"We could tear down the dam, sweetie," Brenda said. "But that won't solve your problems. There's very little water flowing off the mountain; hardly enough to make a difference at this point."

"But if you'd just allow some to pass..."

"Absolutely not!" Bradley barked. "I will not destroy my family's home to save yours. Now, go back to Gaea...or whatever it's called... and leave us be!"

Bradley grabbed his wife's hand and tugged her in the

direction of the dam.

Bub sprang up and over the portly couple, confronting them nose-to-nose. "Hold on a minute," he said. "What if we can promise you that your family will be safe, not just for the next month, but for many months to come?"

Bradley looked at the young frog and chuckled. "What are you going to do, son? Hop up and pull the rain from the clouds?"

"We're going to see Pansophigus," Bub said.

"Ah yes, of course," Bradley mocked. "The all-knowing Pansophigus."

"You know him?"

"I've heard about the arrogant old bird."

"He's got the answers to our problems. He'll know what to do," Bub argued.

"If he knew what to do," said Bradley. "Why hasn't he already done it? Why is he allowing this drought to continue?"

The beaver made a good point, but Bub wasn't about to let Bradley's pessimism rattle the group. If nothing else, the frog and his friends had hope, and no one could take that away.

Bub shivered in the crisp evening air as he held the beaver's gaze.

Abbie unzipped Bub's backpack and pulled out a black thermal windbreaker. "You need your coat, Tadpole. You're already chilly, and it's going to get even colder as we head up the mountain."

"You're actually going to climb Mt. Kirati?" Bradley asked.

"How else will we find Pansophigus?" Bub replied.

"Shoot, frog, that old eagle might not even exist. And even if he does, it's not worth risking your lives to find him."

Brenda shook loose from her husband's hand, annoyed by his stubborn manner.

"We don't have a choice," Alex chimed in. "C'mon, Bub...Abbie...let's go. This puffed-up rat isn't going to cooperate, and it's time for us to find a campsite. We need to be well-rested for tomorrow's climb."

"Why don't you stay here," Brenda suggested.

Bradley started to protest, but his wife's stern expression stopped him in his tracks.

"See that stand of trees just beyond the riverbank," she said. "It'll make a good campsite. And Mt. Kirati's base is only an hour's walk from here. You can head out first thing in the morning."

Brenda scampered over to Alex and stood on her hind legs. "Besides, you look tired, son," she said. "And if you don't get properly clothed, you're going to catch a nasty cold. Your parents would have a fit if they knew you planned on climbing Mt. Kirati in summer attire."

***

"Akina, if you know something, you've got to tell us!" Mayor Chordata and the three young explorers' parents had the flamingo cornered. They were desperate for information.

Abbie's mother approached Akina, waving a folded piece

of crisp white paper.

"Read this, Akina," she wailed. "My daughter and her friends are out there alone; probably in grave danger. Read this, and then tell me you don't know anything."

Akina cautiously accepted the note.

Dear Mom & Dad,

I'm sorry for leaving without asking permission, but I knew you wouldn't allow me to join Alex and Bub on this important quest.

Gaea is our home. It's where we want to grow up and someday raise families of our own. We don't want to live somewhere else. Grandpa Chordata and the other elders decided it was time to pack up and leave, but we can't accept that decision.

We have information that an eagle at the top of Mt. Kirati can provide us with the answers we need. We're going to find him, and we're going to save our town.

There is someone - I won't name her - who will be tracking us. If we get into trouble, we can send a distress signal that will tell her our exact location. I hope that eases any worries you might have.

With a little luck and a lot of determination, the next time we see you, we'll be riding a wave of river water into town.

I love you, and I promise we'll be careful.

Abbie

"Well, those little rascals!" Akina cried, diverting her eyes. "How could they do such a thing?"

"Come now, Akina. We know Abbie was referring to you in the letter," said Mayor Chordata. He twisted his white mustache and glared at the guilt-ridden flamingo. "Septus overheard you talking to the kids. He heard you tell them about Pansophigus."

Akina nervously fluttered her wings and adjusted her rhinestone bifocals. "Alright...okay," she confessed. "It *was* me. But I didn't think they'd actually go search for the old bird. They begged me not to say anything, and let me assure you, I would have spilled the beans if they hadn't given me this." Akina retrieved Bub's device from her pocketbook and offered it to the mayor for inspection.

"I've been tracking the kids since they left town. And they're right on course; about a mile from the base of Mt. Kirati. See this, Mayor?" She pointed to a blinking red dot. "This is their location. Bub invented this gadget, and he has a companion device in his backpack."

"How can you be certain they're not in trouble," Alex's father said as he lumbered toward Akina.

"Now, settle down, Oscar," said Mayor Chordata. He held his hand out, stopping the heated gator in his tracks.

Akina cowered but continued. "They'll probably head up the mountain tomorrow morning. Can't we give them a little more time? They're so close."

"That mountain is treacherous," said Abbie's mother. "They could get hurt, or even..." The salamander buried her head in her husband's chest.

"Akina's right," said Mayor Chordata. "The kids are out of reach for now. Let's give them a chance to succeed."

Abbie's father stroked his wife's head and grumbled, "I think we should go after them right this minute."

The mayor placed a hand on his son's shoulder. "Abbie is your daughter...and my granddaughter. I want to keep her safe just as you do, but I think we owe her the opportunity to achieve this goal."

Mayor Chordata turned to Akina. His face mirrored his son's anxiety.

"We're not happy with your role in this, Akina. You should have warned us about the kids' plan. But we'll take your advice and give them another twenty-four hours. If they're not back in our arms by then, we're going after them."

Chapter Twelve
An Uphill Battle

Daylight peeked over the horizon as Alex sat quietly on a large boulder near the edge of the campsite. The rising sun cast pink shadows on the parched earth, reminding the gator of the colors that once blanketed Gaea; the bright flowers, the dew-clad morning grass and the clear blue waters of a river bursting at the seams. A smile flickered on his long snout.

"That's why we're here," he muttered, careful not to disturb Bub and Abbie. Alex stared at their peaceful faces. It was time to wake them, but he decided to hold off. He needed some quiet time to finalize the day's plans.

Fog-shrouded Mt. Kirati stood high above the tiny campsite. "This isn't going to be easy," Alex grunted, studying the rugged ridges of the intimidating peak. "I'll have to plan our ascent carefully, or we don't stand a chance. Climbing this mountain makes defeating that old goat, Perregrim, look like child's play."

Abbie began to stir. Her eyelids fluttered as she adjusted to the increasing sunlight. "What are you already doing up?" she asked in a voice hoarse with sleep. She rubbed her eyes and raised her arms in a morning stretch.

"Just going over some last minute details," Alex replied, helping Abbie to her feet. "I hope you slept well. It's going to be a tough climb."

"I can handle it," Abbie said. She rolled up her sleeping bag and tapped the still-slumbering Bub on the shoulder. "Time to head up the mountain, Tadpole. We've got an eagle to chat with."

Bub covered his face and begged for five more minutes of sleep, but Abbie was adamant. The young frog sighed, slapped himself on both cheeks, and hopped out of his bedroll. "What's for breakfast?" he croaked.

"Whatever's in your pack," Alex responded. "And let's hope, for our sake, it's not an onion."

Abbie giggled, but was then distracted by the sound of crackling leaves just outside of camp.

"Don't be alarmed. It's just me." Brenda, Bradley's wife, waddled toward them through the dry brush and dropped a stuffed knapsack at their feet. "I couldn't let you head up that mountain without some food and proper clothing," she said. "Bradley and I had some spare winter clothes. You'll need extra layering at the higher altitudes."

"You ain't gonna find anything up there!" Bradley barged into view, followed by his three young kits. "I don't know why you're wastin' your time."

"Bradley!" Brenda barked. "Leave them alone. At least they're trying to find a solution, which is more than I can say for you."

"Arrrgh," the beaver huffed. "You just wait. When they come back empty-handed, you'll start to see things my way."

Alex stomped over to Bradley and pounded his scaly tail on the dry earth. "We're going to climb that mountain, beaver, and get the answers we need. When we come back victorious, you'll eat those words, AND THEN you'll tear down that pile of sticks you call a dam."

"I'm not going to tear down anything until I see some weather changes," Bradley snapped. He stood nose-to-snout with Alex. Neither creature backed down.

"Okay, you two, that's enough!" Abbie shouted. She forced herself between the teeth-bearing pair and pried them apart. "Alex, we need to go. We're losing precious time. And Bradley," she said to the defiant beaver, "if you need solid proof, then maybe you should join us. Although, truth be told, I doubt you have the stamina to keep up."

"I can keep up with you scraggly creatures, no problem!" Bradley snarled. "And I would do it without hesitation if I didn't have a wife and kits to protect."

"We can manage just fine," said Brenda. "It might be good for you to get a little exercise…take off a few of those extra pounds you've packed on."

Brenda waddled over to Abbie and wrapped an arm around her slender frame. "And Bradley," she said, smiling back at her husband. "I'd feel better if these youngsters had an escort; someone familiar with the mountain and its tricky weather conditions."

"But, Brenda," Bradley sputtered, his flat tail slapping

the ground. "I haven't been on that mountain in years. What if I..."

"You'll be fine, dear." Brenda approached her husband, hugged him tightly, and whispered in his ear. "You need this trip, Bradley, for yourself and for the boys. Let them see their father as I remember...strong and fearless. Now go. I'll take good care of the kits. Don't you worry."

Brenda turned to the group and looked reassuringly into each set of nervous eyes. "You're extremely brave for attempting this dangerous journey, and I'm very proud of all of you." She turned to her husband and offered a comforting smile.

The kits hopped up and down, begging for their mother's attention. "Momma! Momma!" they yelped. "Can we go? Can we climb the mountain with Daddy?"

Brenda gathered the boys in her arms and clutched them to her warm belly. "Not quite yet," she whispered. "Someday Daddy will bring you along, but today, I need your help at home. Now do me a favor and fetch Daddy's coat, boots and pack. They're next to the hearth." The kits looked up at their mother, tears of disappointment welling in their big, brown eyes.

"Get moving, boys!" she insisted. "Your father and our guests need to be on their way. Hurry along!"

"Yes, ma'am," they chimed and dashed back to their underwater haven.

Brenda turned back to the anxious climbers. "Open up your packs," she directed. "I want to check your gear. You've got to be properly equipped to scale that mountain."

***

It was still early morning when the group, Bradley included, reached Mt. Kirati's base. The air was frigid, and they huddled together to fight off the chill.

"I...I didn't realize how enormous this mountain was," Bub remarked. He shivered, both from fear and from the brisk wind that whipped them about. He strained his neck to take in the titanic proportions of the great peak. "Are you sure we can do this, Alex?"

"We don't have a choice," Alex responded. "We've come too far to back out now."

"Oh, we can still back out, gator," Bradley growled. "And I think we should seriously consider it. These winds and those approaching clouds signal a storm. Climbing this mountain is a challenge in clear weather. Throw in blizzard conditions and it's virtually impossible."

"Do whatever you like, rodent. But we're moving ahead. Abbie...Bub...put on your heavy coats and climbing boots."

Alex studied the mountainside terrain as the team geared up. The slope directly ahead was dangerously steep and rocky, and with their lack of experience, would be impossible to navigate. But further east, the mountain offered a slightly gentler slope; still a difficult climb, but their chances of reaching the summit would increase.

"Follow me," Alex said.

"Hey, gator, do you know where you're headed?" Bradley asked. "Have you ever been on this mountain?"

"You got any better ideas?" Alex yelled. The howling wind grabbed his words and hurled them at the insulting beaver. "You do a lot of complaining but not a lot of contributing."

Bradley stopped to look up at the dark, threatening sky. A tiny snowflake drifted down, landed on the tip of his black nose and quickly melted away. "Go figure," he said, ignoring Alex's snide comment. "It hasn't snowed the past two winters, and the day we decide to climb this mountain, here it comes!"

Perhaps it was the pristine snowflake that softened his demeanor, but Bradley suddenly felt the need to make peace. He approached Alex and offered his hand. "You're right, gator," he said. "If we're going to survive this mountain, we've got to band together. My buddies and I attempted to climb this bear several times. We never made it to the summit, but we got close. If you'll let me lead the way, I think I'll soon have my mountain legs back. Deal?"

"Deal," Alex replied, clutching the beaver's outstretched hand.

***

Bradley led the troop up the eastern slope. "You were headed in the right direction," he yelled back to the alligator. "This route will be less difficult, but it won't be easy. Stay on my tail and keep an eye on Abbie and Bub."

"Got it," Alex replied.

Snow began to swirl around the group. Alex worried that his friends, more accustomed to the tropical environment of Gaea, would have trouble adjusting. But Abbie and Bub were hanging tough and seemed to be handling the rocky terrain without much difficulty. He checked on them anyway.

"How are you two holding up?"

"We're fine," Abbie replied. "But speak up. We're having trouble hearing you. The winds are really picking up, and the snow is cutting visibility. Don't get too far ahead, okay?"

"I won't, Abbie, I promise."

Bradley's anxiety increased as a heavier bank of clouds rolled in. The storm strengthened, and the mountain's slope grew steep. The beaver tugged his wooly cap over his ears and paused to allow the others to catch up.

"What's going on?" Bub asked as the group gathered around. "Why are we stopping?"

"This isn't looking good," Bradley replied. "The storm is getting worse, and I'm concerned about the rough terrain. We should consider heading back down. If the weather clears up, we can take another shot at the mountain tomorrow."

"You don't understand," Alex bellowed over the howling wind. "We're running out of time! If we don't get to Pansophigus by tomorrow morning, this trip will all be for nothing!"

"We can do this, Bradley," Abbie cried. The snow, now coming down in sheets, stung her face like a thousand tiny needles. "You're either with us, or you're not. Which is it?"

Bradley nervously nibbled on a walking stick while his broad tail packed down the drifting snow. "I can't let you do this alone, not in these conditions," Bradley shouted. "Besides, Brenda would have my pelt if I came back alone."

"Then let's get going," Alex urged. "We're running out of time."

***

"Stay in sight!" Alex yelled to Abbie and Bub. "I'll drag my tail. It'll create a wider path in the snow behind me."

Blizzard conditions quickly enveloped the tiring mountaineers, and a shivering Abbie grabbed Bub's hand, pulling him close. "Get in front of me," she yelled in his ear. "Try to follow in Alex's wake. And hold onto me…don't let go!"

The tiny frog was beginning to falter. The snow now reached his belly and crept under his heavy coat and sweater, chilling him to the core. Each step was a struggle, but the exhausted Bub trudged ahead. His bulky scarf whipped behind him, continually popping Abbie in the face.

"Alex, slow down!" she shouted.

Alex peered back through the heavy snow. Bub and Abbie were less than ten feet behind, but he could barely make them out. The alligator grabbed Bradley by the coat and turned toward his friends. "We're right here," he called out. "Follow my voice until you see us!"

Bub pushed forward. To keep the strong winds from separating them, Abbie grabbed one of the frog's backpack straps. The snow was up to Bub's chest and getting deeper by the minute. "I can't do this anymore, Abbie," he yelped, exhausted. "You three go ahead. I'll find a place to rest…" The young frog's voice trailed off as he tumbled, face-first, into the billowy snow.

"Bub, get up!" Abbie screamed. "I won't leave you. You can't stop now; not in this storm!" Abbie pulled him to her chest. He was shivering uncontrollably, and his once green skin had turned a deep shade of blue. She opened her parka and wrapped it around the semi-conscious frog. Through the swirling snow, she caught sight of Alex heading back their way. His steps were slow and labored, his limbs made heavy by the treacherous conditions.

"You've got to keep moving, Abbie," he shouted. "The snow is piling up around you!"

"I can't," she cried. "It's up to my waist. It's too heavy. And I can't leave Bub!"

Alex fought desperately to reach his two pals, each step requiring more effort than the last.

From behind the struggling alligator, Bradley popped into view wielding a small shovel in his stout arms. "Brenda insisted I pack this darn thing," he shouted. "I thought she was nuts for loading me down with unnecessary items. But, as usual, she was right." He shoveled his way past Alex, digging a path to Abbie and Bub. They reached the frightened salamander and lethargic frog moments later.

"He's in bad shape, Alex," Abbie wailed. She held Bub in a tight embrace. "We've got to get him warm, now!"

"Let's huddle together below that big rock," Bradley yelled, pointing to a large boulder several feet away. "There's nowhere else to go at this point. The conditions are too severe to climb further up or head back. We'll just have to wait out the storm and hope it dies down soon."

"Abbie, take my hand and keep hold of Bub. I'll pull you along," Alex instructed. "I'll follow behind you, Bradley. Clear a path to that rock."

The beaver immediately began to shovel the drifting snow. His short arms moved like pistons and his quick breaths trailed behind him in the cold mountain air.

"It's getting worse," he grunted. "We'll be lucky if we make it to the rock!"

Alex stumbled past the tired beaver. Using his last bit of energy, he waved his arms and tail wildly, creating a temporary path to the boulder. Bradley grabbed Abbie and Bub and dragged them behind him. "Get up against the rock and huddle close together," he yelled. "We'll use our body heat to keep from freezing."

Abbie shook Bub as she nestled close to the others. "Wake up, Tadpole," she screamed. "You've got to wake up!" The weak frog slowly opened his heavy lids and stared blankly at the frightened salamander. "It's going to be okay," she whispered, hugging him tightly. "We're going to be just fine." She glanced at Alex for reassurance, and for the first time in her life, saw fear in his eyes.

"Alex?"

"The storm's not letting up, Abbie," he said, wrapping his

arms around her. "I'm sorry. I shouldn't have brought you here. I'm so sorry."

"No, Alex!" she yelped. "Don't...don't you do that! We're going to make it. We didn't come all this way to freeze up on this mountain. I won't allow it!" Exhausted by her outburst and short of breath from the high altitude, Abbie curled up against Alex and cradled Bub in her arms. "I simply won't allow it," she whimpered.

Ten minutes passed before Abbie spoke again. "It's so cold," she muttered. The snow continued to pile around them. They were no longer able to push it aside. "Alex? Bradley?" her weak voice called out. There was no response.

Minutes passed like hours as Abbie fought the urge to close her eyes. She huddled close to the others, trying to keep them warm. In the distance, she spotted movement. "Hello?" Her voice was hoarse and weak. "Is someone out there?" Her eyes fluttered as she struggled to stay awake. She squinted to make out an approaching figure, not sure if she were dreaming.

"No!" she cried out as a monstrous creature came into full view. The beast let out a loud roar and swept the group from under the boulder, corralling them in one of its giant, furry arms. Alex, Bub and Bradley lay limp in its grasp, but Abbie kicked and screamed, attempting to free herself and the others. Each movement caused the creature to squeeze tighter. "HELP!" she screamed through a flurry of tears.

"LET THEM GO, YOU OVERSIZED APE!" A voice squealed over the storm's howling winds. Abbie heard a loud, buzzing noise. She craned her neck to find the source, but heavy snow beat against her face, clouding her vision.

Their captor ignored the interruption and moved effortlessly through the driving snow and bone-chilling wind, carrying the crew toward a large cave.

"Help! Help us!" Abbie cried. The buzzing grew louder. Something, or someone, was in hot pursuit of the beast that held them.

"I SAID LEAVE THEM BE!" a suddenly familiar voice screeched. A lightning-fast blur dove at the burly monster. The creature swung its free arm, narrowly missing the relentless insect that had now come into view.

"PTERON!" Abbie screamed. "Pteron, is that really you?"

"It's me, Abbie. I'm here!" The bundled dragonfly huffed as he circled his surprisingly agile foe. "Is everyone okay? How's Bub?"

"Not good, Pteron," she wailed. "You've got to save us!"

The insect took a deep breath and again dove at the massive snow giant. Time was running out. The creature was closing in on a dark cave, and Pteron's rescue attempts had done little more than agitate his foe.

"Pteron, be careful!" Abbie cried just as the hairy beast dealt the dragonfly a powerful blow. Pteron crashed into a snow bank near the cave's entrance and disappeared into its powdery depths.

Chapter Thirteen
The Tuwakis

Pteron lay outside as the blizzard continued its pounding. The drifting snow covered his motionless body and blocked entry to the cave.

Inside, the creature's long white fur dripped melting snow on his unresponsive captives. A small fire flickered on the cold dirt floor. Its flames cast grotesque shadows, magnifying the snow monster's size.

"Wake up," he growled, bearing a row of crooked yellow teeth. He moved in closer to check for signs of movement. There were none. "I waited too long," he mumbled. "The boss will have my hide for this."

"What...what's going on," a weak voice muttered.

Startled by the unexpected noise, the oversized ogre exposed razor-sharp claws and eyed the cave's entrance. He saw nothing but a wall of packed snow. The noise was coming from inside the cave.

The tiny voice spoke again. "Where am I?" It was Bub. He was beginning to stir.

The creature turned toward his captives and bent over

the frog, carefully inspecting his condition.

Bub pulled his legs out from under a blanket of weaved straw, knocked his bulky ear muffs aside, and rubbed his eyes. Only then did he spot the frightening figure above him. "Who are you?" Bub croaked, stumbling from his makeshift bed and feebly hopping toward the nearest dark corner. "What do you want?"

Bub's frightened words bounced off the drab stone walls, creating a loud echo and jarring the others from their slumber. Alex slowly rolled from side to side. His ridged tail swept across the hard cave floor. Bradley and Abbie also awakened, but were dazed and unsure of their whereabouts.

"Alex, help!" Bub screeched.

"Huh? What? Who's calling for me?" Alex floated between consciousness and a fuzzy dream state. "Abbie?" he mumbled. "Abbie, is that you?" Concern for his friend quickly snapped the alligator out of his haze. He tossed the straw blanket that covered him into the fire. The tiny flame suddenly flared, licking at the cave's damp ceiling. The increased light revealed Abbie's location, and Alex rushed to her side, still unaware of the monster lurking in the shadows.

"Abbie, wake up," Alex pleaded as he gently shook the groggy salamander.

"Are we okay?" she asked, her voice hardly more than a whisper.

Alex smiled and brushed a strand of hair away from her face.

"Where are we, Alex?" she whimpered.

"ALEX!" Bub again screamed. "Look behind you!"

The alligator turned in the direction of the frog's desperate cry and found him cornered by a being so colossal its shaggy head scraped the cave's ceiling.

"BACK AWAY FROM THE FROG!" Alex yelled. He pushed Abbie and the befuddled Bradley in the direction of the cave's entrance.

"Stay there," he ordered. "I've got to help Bub."

"Alex!" Abbie called out. "Promise me you'll be careful."

"Don't worry about me," Alex said. He lunged at the hairy beast, sinking a snout full of sharp gator teeth into its thick leg.

The creature howled in pain. "HANG ON A MINUTE!" it roared, swatting at the firmly attached alligator. "I'M NOT HERE TO HARM YOU!"

Alex continued to hang on, but loosened his bite. The monster took a deep breath to calm its nerves. "Kindly unclamp your teeth, alligator, and let me speak."

Alex reluctantly released his grip but did not back away. "You've got ten seconds to explain yourself," he snarled.

"My name is Boreas," the creature quickly responded. "I was sent by Pansophigus to rescue you."

"I don't understand," Abbie said from across the deep cave. "Why didn't you say something before, when you grabbed us outside?"

"The conditions were horrible," said Boreas, his voice now gentle and comforting. "I had enough trouble locating your group, much less explaining who I was. And when I found you, things didn't look so good. You were freezing, all of you. You needed warmth, not idle chit chat." Boreas paused briefly to rub his throbbing leg. "And then some pesky dragonfly started dive-bombing me. Hard to believe," he said, shaking his great mane. "Whoever heard of a dragonfly buzzing around in a blizzard?"

"Dragonfly!" Bub yelped. "What dragonfly?"

"Oh, no!" Abbie shrieked. Her last memories outside the cave came flooding back. "Pteron was out there! He was trying to help us!"

"You know that pesky bug?" Boreas asked. "I thought he was trying to hurt you. I didn't realize..."

"Hurry!" Abbie cried. "We've got to find him. He should be near the entrance, where Boreas slapped him aside."

Bub glared at the snow creature, his eyes filled with anger and worry. "You did what?" he croaked.

The gentle giant cast his eyes downward. "I didn't know..."

"I don't want to hear it," Bub interrupted. "Pteron is out there alone, in the cold. We can't waste anymore time. Let's go get him!"

Boreas lumbered toward the cave's entrance, followed by all but Bradley. The snow was beginning to push its way inside.

Boreas jammed his arm through the wall of white, blindly searching for the insect. "No luck," he said. "There's nothing there."

"I'm breaking out of here," Bub cried. "We can't abandon Pteron. He risked his life to help us; we owe him the same consideration."

"No, Bub," said Abbie, grabbing the frantic frog. "You're in no condition to go outside. You wouldn't last two minutes in that storm."

"But Abbie, we can't just let him freeze," Bub sobbed.

"Ahhh, quit your blubbering, frog," said a muffled voice. A flurry of snowflakes filled the cave's entrance, and four miniscule hiking boots pushed through a jagged hole. "Grab my feet and pull me through. C'mon folks, what does a dragonfly have to do to get a little help around here?"

"Pteron!" Bub cheered. He took hold of his old pal's boots and pulled him into the warm cave. The shivering insect, dressed in full arctic gear, collapsed in the frog's arms.

"Hey, little buddy!" Bub cried, dancing around the cave.

"Take it easy, pal," the jostled insect grumbled. "Let a guy gather his wits."

Bub chuckled heartily and enveloped his friend in an enthusiastic hug.

"Bring him over here, close to the fire," Boreas said. "We've got to raise his body temperature. Take off those wet boots and wrap him in one of the straw blankets."

Pteron turned toward the strange voice. His eyes grew wide with fear. "AHHHHH!" he screamed. "Run! Run for your lives! It's the beast!"

Bradley, still in a fuzzy haze, reacted to the confused dragonfly's alarmed cry. "DO AS HE SAYS! RUN!" He raced toward the cave's entrance and blasted through the wall of snow to the outside.

"What in the world...what's gotten into that crazy rodent?" Abbie said. "Go get him, Alex. Give him a good shake, and bring him back to reality."

Alex reached through the cave's entrance, grabbed Bradley by his flat tail and pulled him back inside.

"That buck-toothed beaver has the right idea," Pteron cried, suspiciously eyeing the giant. "What's wrong with all of you? Don't you realize you're in a cave with a monster!"

"Pteron, Boreas is on our side," said Bub. "He was sent by Pansophigus to help us."

"That *helpful* beast almost put me six feet under," Pteron replied. "If I hadn't been properly attired, he..."

"Oh, Alex, look!" Abbie interrupted. She pointed to the Bradley-shaped hole in the snow at the cave's entrance. Rays of sunlight poured through, illuminating the once dark cavern. "The sun's out! The storm is over!"

"Then let's get going," Alex said. "We need to find Pansophigus before sunset."

"Not so fast," said Boreas. "You folks need to eat some food and rest for awhile. I'll take you to Pansophigus once you've regained some strength."

"One hour," Alex insisted. "That's as long as we can wait."

Boreas escorted the impatient gator over to the fire and offered him a steaming cup of hot tea. "An hour it is."

***

Boreas insisted on carrying his new friends to Mt. Kirati's summit. The fiercely independent group fought the idea, but the snow giant was adamant. He would carry them, or they wouldn't go at all. The crew gave in.

Bub and Alex perched on Boreas' broad shoulders, while Bradley and Abbie snuggled in the warmth of his furry arms. But Pteron, still leery of the creature's intentions, insisted on hovering just out of reach.

The spring blizzard had passed like a thief in the night, dumping six feet of snow in just over three hours. As a result, the warmth of the afternoon sun, now high in the clear blue sky, created a new hazard...melting snow. But the team was safe with Boreas at the helm, and in just over an hour, they caught their first glimpse of Mt. Kirati's awe-inspiring summit.

"It's beautiful," Abbie gasped.

Boreas stopped momentarily, allowing his passengers to appreciate the snow-draped peak. The sun's rays created a natural spotlight, guiding the excited crew to the destination they'd fought so hard to reach.

"I see something on the mountain's tip," Abbie continued. "Is that Pansophigus?"

"No, Abbie, that's his nest," Boreas said. "But I can assure you, he'll be there soon. He's anxious to meet all of you."

"What do you think, Bradley," Alex said to the unusually silent beaver. "Still believe Pansophigus is a figment of our imaginations?"

Bradley didn't immediately respond. The mountain's rugged peak captivated him. It was his first time to the summit, and he wanted to drink in the experience. "If only Brenda and the kits were here to enjoy this with me," he muttered.

Alex reached down from his perch and playfully yanked on the bill of Bradley's cap. "Quite a sight, huh, beaver? Aren't you glad you joined us?" Bradley grabbed the gator's hand and gave it a hearty shake.

Alex turned to Boreas. "I hope you'll allow us to walk from here. It's important that we approach Pansophigus on our own."

They were just moments from the summit. Pansophigus' nest was less than a hundred feet away. "I understand," Boreas replied. "But let me clear a path. The snow is still quite deep and becoming a bit slushy."

"Fair enough. Thank you, buddy."

The giant bent down and gently placed Abbie and Bradley in the tracks behind him. Alex and Bub jumped to the ground near their friends, and Pteron climbed onto Bub's shoulder. "I think I'll ride the rest of the way in my favorite spot," Pteron chirped. "That is, if you don't mind, frog."

"Wouldn't have it any other way, Ace," Bub cheerfully replied. "I've carried you this far. Might as well lug you the rest of the way."

Without warning, the young mountaineers felt a powerful gust of wind and caught a flash of something magnificent.

Boreas turned back to the group. "It's Pansophigus!"

Abbie's heart fluttered, and her eyes welled up with

tears. "We made it," she whispered. "We actually made it."

A steep incline stood between the group and a hefty boulder that lay just below the great eagle's nest. Delicate clouds masked the peak, but a gentle breeze soon nudged them away. Abbie stood spellbound as the great Pansophigus appeared. He stood tall in his massive nest. The blazing sun outlined his magnificent silhouette, and his giant wings, spread wide, welcomed his guests from their long journey. The young explorers were awed by his presence. They struggled, but succeeded in climbing on top of the boulder just below the regal bird.

"My courageous friends," his powerful voice boomed. "I am so very proud to welcome you to my home; to the very apex of beautiful Mt. Kirati."

Pteron felt faint in the eagle's presence and latched onto Bub's heavy scarf for support. The others stood entranced, not yet believing that they stood in the presence of Kirati's legendary eagle; the very one they'd heard about in ancient stories passed down from one generation to the next.

"He really does exist," Alex muttered. "My hero exists."

Pansophigus dropped his majestic wings. "Yes, Alex," he said. "I do exist. But I'm no hero. All of you standing before me...you're the heroes."

"Oh, no, sir, we're not heroes," Abbie respectfully objected, bowing in front of the great eagle. "We've simply come to seek your advice."

"Abbie," Pansophigus said, gingerly placing a wing tip on her golden head. "Please, stand up. I am not to be revered.

I'm just an old eagle; wise, some might say, but an old bird nonetheless." He stared directly into the eyes of each proud explorer. "Am I to understand that you've come to me for solutions to save your home?"

They nodded in unison. Pansophigus smiled and continued. "The great river you followed to the base of Mt. Kirati...was it polluted before you started your journey?" he asked.

"Yes, it was," they answered.

"Is it now?"

"No, sir," Alex answered.

"Did I lead you into the *Swamp of Despair* to collect the willow tears? How about Perregrim, did I destroy his evil mind-control plan or free his poor prisoners? And Bradley's river dam...did I tell you where to find it?"

"No, sir," Alex again replied.

"During this journey, you faced many obstacles." Pansophigus adjusted the spectacles resting on his prominent beak. "Not once was I there to counsel you. And do you know why?"

"Why, sir?" Bub asked.

Pansophigus dropped a wing and gently swept up the frog. "Because you didn't need me," he said, smiling proudly. "The determination inside each of you was all you required."

Pansophigus sat the elated frog back down and Abbie stepped forward. "You're right, sir. We cleaned up the pollution and discovered at least one reason for the river's meager flow, but we haven't solved the bigger problem," she said. "There's simply not enough water to replenish Gaea's lagoon."

"I'm afraid, sir, that I've been part of the problem," Bradley said, waddling forward, his head hung low.

"Don't be ashamed of your role in this," said Pansophigus. "You were doing what was necessary to take care of your family. Beavers don't control nature, and neither do I. But what we can do is cooperate with each other; work together to solve our common problems. I have confidence that you will do that in the future."

Bradley looked up at the kind eagle. "I will, I promise."

Pansophigus then addressed Abbie. "Nature has an amazing ability to replenish itself, Abbie. But there are times when it can be unpredictable, such as now."

"So, are you telling me we came all this way for nothing," Abbie said, her frustration mounting. "Everything…all we've risked…doesn't mean a thing?"

"Oh, it means a great deal, Abbie," said the wise eagle. "We can't control Mother Nature, but we can control how we use her resources."

"With all due respect, sir," Abbie interjected. "What in the world can we do about a lack of snow or rain?"

Alex tugged Abbie's arm, concerned that she would offend the great eagle. "Abbie, please," he whispered. "You've said enough."

"Her question is valid, Alex, and it deserves an answer. But it won't be a simple one. I'll get to that momentarily, Abbie, but first…" Pansophigus reached deep into his nest and pulled out five gold medallions dangling from elegant blue ribbons.

"Please step forward, all of you." One by one, the eagle placed a medal around the neck of each proud explorer. "I bestow these medals upon you to acknowledge your strength of character and courage on this mission to save your home."

Pteron stared at the golden pendant whose weight had nearly caused him to tumble from Bub's shoulder to the slushy snow below. He read the inscription out loud. "The Tuwakis: May they always fight for nature's precious gifts." The dragonfly looked again at Pansophigus. "Who are the Tuwakis, sir?"

"If you choose," the eagle replied. "*You* are the Tuwakis. All of you." He swept a wing across the sky to signify the group as a whole. "But this title is not to be taken lightly. The natives of this region had a great respect for nature. They devoted their lives to honoring and preserving its many gifts. That's why I chose this name, Pteron. To those caring souls, the word "tuwaki" signified 'earth' and 'rain'. To you, it signifies a long-term mission and a dedication to the natural world around you."

The small band stood proud as they listened to the eagle's words. They had battled great odds and were now being recognized for their successes...by the great Pansophigus, no less!

"During the past week, you've displayed uncommon courage," the eagle continued. "I challenge you to now impart great wisdom. Teach your families, friends, and communities the importance of preserving and respecting each of nature's wonderful offerings. Take to them the knowledge I offer you...knowledge that will serve you well even in desperate times such as these."

"Please, sir," Bub pleaded. "Tell us everything you know."

Pansophigus chuckled at the young frog's eager request. "I wish I could tell you everything," he said to the group. "Unfortunately, we don't have that kind of time. Your families are worried. You need to head for home. But don't fret, you're not leaving empty-handed."

Pansophigus reached into his nest once again and lifted out a thick, worn book. Its brown leather cover was warped and cracking; its pages dog-eared from countless years of use. The eagle bent forward and carefully placed the book in Abbie's arms.

"What's in the book, Mister Pansophigus? Is it magical?"

"No, Abbie. There's nothing magical about respecting our planet; about conserving its resources. The book simply contains information on how earth's creatures can live in harmony with nature. Study it well. Teach your fellow Tuwakis its many lessons and encourage them to teach others."

Abbie looked up at the proud eagle. Tears glistened in her eyes. "I'm so sorry for doubting you," she said. "For challenging your wisdom."

"Don't be," the eagle replied. "That same inquisitive nature will make you a great leader and a wonderful caretaker of your environment." Pansophigus turned to the others. "Take note, my friends. The blizzard that seemed such a hurdle was, in truth, a gift from nature. The bright sun which now warms our bodies will melt a significant amount of this snow before nightfall."

"And the water will flow down the mountain to the river!" Bub cried.

"That's right, Bub," Pansophigus chuckled. "It won't solve all of your problems, but it's a start. The rest is up to you."

***

The bright afternoon sun continued its slow descent as Pansophigus chatted with his guests, answering their questions and offering advice for success in their new role. Bub dabbled in the tiny rivulets of water flowing around his feet. "The snow is really melting fast," he said.

"It's springtime," said Pansophigus from his regal perch. "The afternoon hours bring temperatures well above freezing. In fact, you should take leave before the melting snow turns into flowing streams." The eagle turned to Boreas. "Old friend, please escort the Tuwakis down the western slope. Place them in a hollowed-out log where the snow rivulets converge with the river. You'll need to leave now, so they can be home before nightfall."

"Climb aboard," Boreas said. "Let's get down this slope!"

Abbie and her friends bade Pansophigus a heartfelt goodbye and hopped aboard the shaggy creature's massive frame. Pteron returned to Bub's shoulder, and as their escort began his rapid descent, the little dragonfly let out a joyful cry. "WAHOO, IT'S TIME TO GO HOME!!"

Unlike the treacherous trip up Mt. Kirati, the journey downhill was magical. Boreas knew every inch of the rugged mountain, and navigated its tricky terrain and increasing snowmelt with ease. To the Tuwakis, it was like riding a gentle, winding roller coaster.

"We're nearing the mountain's base," Boreas said. He slowed to a brisk walk and pointed toward the converging waters. "Take a look at that; the river is flowing again." The furry beast dropped to one knee. "Time to unload. Pteron, why don't you circle the area and find us a sizable log to hollow out. You guys will have to float it downriver without me."

"Why, Boreas?" Bub asked as he used the creature's scraggly white fur to swing to the earth below. "Why don't you go with us? How long has it been since you visited the flatlands?"

"I can't leave the shelter of the mountain," the gentle giant replied. "You five are the first to catch sight of me in years. In fact, most flatlanders question the very existence of Mt. Kirati's snow monster. I'd like to keep it that way."

"Maybe you just don't want folks to know what a kind soul you are," Abbie teased.

"You're right, little lady," Boreas playfully growled as he placed the salamander on the mountainside. "I don't want to destroy my 'mysterious' image."

"Where's Pteron," Alex cut in. "We need that log. We only have a few more hours of daylight."

"I'm right above you, gator," Pteron buzzed. "The blizzard took down some old trees. There's a nice-sized one about ten paces to your left. Get that toothy beaver over there to hollow it out."

"Good thing Brenda loaded me down with all these tools," Bradley said, poking into his pack. He pulled out a pick axe and handed it to Boreas. "You start on one end of the tree, big guy, and I'll take the other. These big buck-teeth aren't just for show. We'll have us a boat in no time." A mere twenty minutes later, the dust settled and Bradley and Boreas stepped aside to reveal a neatly hollowed log.

"Great work," Alex commented. He rifled through the debris surrounding the crude little boat and picked up several long strips of bark. "We'll use these for paddles."

"Ah, you land dwellers," Pteron teased, circling just above their heads. "If only you had wings; maybe you wouldn't be so much trouble to deal with."

"Clam it, Ace," Alex replied. He gave the mouthy insect a playful swat and then turned to Boreas. "My friend," he said, holding out his hand. "I'd like to thank you for what you did. If it weren't for you…"

"No thanks needed," Boreas interrupted. He took the alligator's outstretched hand and shook it heartily. "You would have done the same for me. Of that, I'm certain. Now get out of here!"

Abbie wrapped her arms around the snow creature's leg while the others waved an enthusiastic goodbye.

"Ouch! Careful, little one," Boreas yelped. "You're squeezing right where that gator bit into me. He sure knows how to make a point."

Abbie giggled and released her grip. "We love you, Boreas," she whispered and dashed off to join her friends at the river.

Pteron perched in the front of the log, proclaiming himself captain. "To the oars, men...and Abbie," he shouted as the crew lifted the rig from the ground. "Today we ride!"

***

Alex and Bub took a seat in the log's hollowed-out cavity and held their breath. "It works," Bub exclaimed as the makeshift boat gently bobbed under their weight. "It really floats!"

"Alright, Abbie...Bradley," Alex said. "Hop in. The river's flowing well. Once I shove off, the current will take us downstream very quickly. Is everyone ready?"

"Ready!" They cried in unison. Alex pushed the log away from the riverbank and hopped in. They were on their way.

Behind them, rivulets of melted snow joined together to form streams that poured into the rising river. With each coupling, the current grew stronger, and the log's speed increased. It wasn't long before Bradley's dam appeared in the distance.

"There it is," the excited beaver shouted. Four tiny figures hopped up and down on top of the mound. "Look, it's Brenda and the kits." Bradley turned away to hide tears of joy.

"Daddy! Daddy!" the stout little beavers screamed. "Momma, here comes Daddy! He's riding in a log."

The boat soon entered a placid body of water gathering behind the dam. "Bradley," Alex said to the emotional beaver. "Your dam is creating quite a lake. I'm afraid it's time to tear down a portion of the barrier to let the river flow through. Are you willing to do that?"

"You bet I am," Bradley replied, remembering the great eagle's words. "In the spirit of cooperation, we'll knock out a good chunk of it. But first, let me hug that family of mine."

The crew docked their crude boat next to the structure. Bradley hopped out and ran to Brenda and the three excited kits. "I knew you could do it," Brenda cried as she clung tightly to her husband. "I just knew it!"

"What's this, Daddy?" one of the kits chirped, inspecting the shiny gold medallion hanging from his father's neck.

"Who are the Tu-wa-kis?" another asked, sounding out the strange word.

"I'll explain it all later this evening, boys," Bradley said. "Right now, we need to help the others." Bradley turned to Brenda, who still had a protective arm around her husband. "We've got to remove part of the dam," he said.

"But Bradley, what about our home?"

"Don't worry, honey. We'll save that portion, but the rest has to go. If there's more snowfall and enough snowmelt, we'll soon be able to relocate to a nearby stream."

"That brave group of youngsters was determined to save their home, and in the process, they helped countless other families," Brenda said. "It's only fair that we take down the barrier."

"I knew you'd understand." Bradley smiled and hugged his wife before diving into the cool water and swimming toward the others. Brenda and the kits followed close behind.

The beavers emerged from the rising river, shook off their wet fur, and joined the rest of the team. "We'll need to carry the logs and other debris off to one side," Bradley instructed. "Let's form an assembly line. We can pass the pieces to each other and finish this chore in no time." The crew quickly positioned themselves along the dam toward the eastern bank of the river.

Pteron shouted words of encouragement from above as the team tore away large chunks, careful not to disturb the family's underground home.

"Go! Go! Go!" the dragonfly chanted. "The faster you move, the faster you get home!"

Bub scooped up a handful of river water and tossed it at the hovering dragonfly. Pteron dove to miss the droplets and took a couple of buzzing laps around the frog's head. Bub howled with laughter as Pteron continued his goofy cheers.

"We're almost there," Bradley yelled. A steady stream of water had begun to flow over the dam. "It's getting dark. The four of you need to get in that boat and head downstream. Brenda and I will finish up here.

Abbie grabbed one last bundle of muddy sticks and tossed them to Bub. "Bradley's right," she said. "It's time to go home."

***

Back in Gaea, Akina and Mayor Chordata gathered the townsfolk around the lagoon. The air was electric and the town was buzzing with excitement.

"Akina's tracking device shows the kids heading our way," the mayor shouted. "We're also seeing signs of clear, fresh water flowing into the lagoon."

"HOORAY!" the myriad of creatures shouted. Steady streams of clear water began to pour over the ledge high above the lagoon. Gaea's beautiful waterfall had returned.

"It appears our courageous young explorers have accomplished their mission," Mayor Chordata continued. "Let's give them the hearty welcome they deserve!" The crowd rushed home and quickly returned to the lagoon with baskets of food and drink, colorful balloons and streamers, and a giant "Welcome Home" sign.

"They're just around the bend," the mayor cried, taking one last glance at Akina's tracking device. "Look at the fresh water pouring in! It's unbelievable!"

Moments later, a surge of water poured over the ledge and into the lagoon. It carried with it a hollow log containing the town's precious cargo. Pteron circled high above, observing the magnificent homecoming, while Alex, Bub and Abbie leaped from their boat and plunged into the lagoon below. They quickly resurfaced, arms raised in victory. "We're home!" they cried. "We're home!"

For the first time in over a year, the joyous creatures of Gaea dove into their beloved lagoon. It would be awhile before the lush foliage would return, but the town's hopes for the future, along with their sparkling water, had been restored. They swept up their young heroes, lifted them high above their heads, and shouted, "HOORAY! HOORAY!"

Epilogue

"Where are you off to, pumpkin," Akina drawled, stepping in front of Abbie. "You better not be takin' off again without tellin' your parents."

In the three months since Abbie, Bub and Alex's homecoming, the tourists had returned in full force. The flamboyant flamingo, Akina, dressed in full tropical attire and trailed by three energetic photo-snapping seals, had resumed her old tour guide gig. "You look like you're up to somethin'."

"No, ma'am," Abbie replied. "I'm just going for a walk."

"You're off to that tree of yours, aren't ya? You and your buddies have been so busy teachin' us how to conserve water, I bet you haven't had a moment to yourself."

"That's right," Abbie replied. "I'm just trying to squeeze in some quiet time."

Peeking around the flamingo, the seals snuck in several more photos of the shy salamander.

"You kids are quite the attraction these days," Akina said. Abbie twirled a lock of hair around her finger, embarrassed by the attention. Akina motioned for the seals to back off. "Can't really blame 'em for being interested, hon.

Everyone wants to meet the younguns...the Tuwakis...who defeated the horrible Perregrim and stood in the presence of the great eagle, Pansophigus."

"Yes, I know," Abbie sighed. She dutifully waved to the star-struck seals who immediately snapped more photos. "I think I'll get going, Akina," she said. "See you later." Abbie was anxious to escape the chaos and take refuge in the solace of her giant Banyan tree. From a distance, she marveled at its massive canopy, reaching high above the blossoming landscape. Summer's humid air and occasional rain showers had restored its regal posture, and its branches sprouted evergreen leaves by the thousands.

Oh, and Abbie, I cut my mornin' shower down to five minutes," Akina called out as the young salamander hurried away. "Whatcha think about that?"

"I think you saved the town another twenty-five gallons of water," Abbie answered, refusing to turn back. "And you're just as beautiful as ever!"

The flamingo smiled, fluffed her bright pink feathers, and shuffled her camera-toting guests toward the lagoon. "The flowers on the east end of the lagoon are simply mahhhvelous...."

***

Abbie approached the outer boundary of her ancient sanctuary. Waves of emotion washed through her, and she breathed deeply to calm her nerves. A low-hanging branch swayed before her in the gentle summer breeze. She reached out, grabbed hold of it, and waved its dark, green leaves under her long snout. They smelled fresh and inviting. Abbie released the branch and moved into the shade of the tree's lush umbrella. The banyan's intricate root system, weaving into and out of the ground like a giant needle and thread, created maze-like corridors. She zigzagged among them, finally reaching the tree's enormous hollow trunk. Abbie reached inside and removed the treasure she had placed there months before. She sat the weathered wooden box down beside her and leaned against the sturdy tree, savoring her privacy. It wasn't long before the peaceful surroundings lulled the exhausted salamander into a deep slumber.

"Abbie, are you back there?" Alex called out, waking her from her peaceful nap. He was still dripping wet from his latest antics in the lagoon. "You've been gone for hours. We were getting worried."

Abbie rubbed her eyes and grabbed onto a Banyan limb, pulling herself up. "No reason to worry," she smiled. "I was just taking care of something."

"Oh, yeah?" Alex glanced at the object Abbie now held in her hands. "What's with the box?"

"Ah, nothing," she replied. "You wouldn't be interested."

The young gator shrugged his shoulders, comfortable with the reality that he would never fully understand Abbie's secretive ways. "Alright then," he said, sweeping his heavy tail through the lush grass. "Let's get back to town before your parents send out a search party." Abbie smiled and blushed as

Alex grabbed her free hand to guide her back to town.

"I need to run home," she said as they neared the sparkling lagoon crowded with tourists, townspeople…and her parents. "I'll be back in a few minutes." Abbie dropped Alex's hand and waved to her parents who shook their heads in frustration.

"Abbie, please tell your father or me when you're going off somewhere," her mother shouted. "We still haven't recovered from your trip up that mountain."

"Okay, Mom," Abbie replied. "I'm just going home for a bit. I won't be long."

Once there, Abbie ran straight to her room. She closed the door and placed the wooden box on her dresser.

"Time to put these objects in their rightful place," she mused. Abbie opened the lid and, one by one, pulled out the memories she'd put there…memories of days she thought would never return. But they had.

She returned the water lily painting to the hook on her pink wall and placed the small globe and pictures back on her dresser. She twirled a lock of golden hair as she stared at the crude lettering on the box's lid: *A Tribute to Home.*

Abbie grabbed her grandfather's pocketknife and carefully scraped away the words. She then walked to her bedside table and pulled out the worn book Pansophigus had given her. She placed it in the box and closed the lid. Using the same pocketknife, she meticulously etched something new, then stood back to view her handiwork. She smiled, pleased by the appearance of the simple, but clear letters, which read: *The Tuwakis.*